"Do you think you've got what you need?"

Alice looked out into the darkness to where the Indian Ocean boomed beyond the reef.

"I've got a career," she said, ignoring the little voice that said it wasn't much of one at the moment. "I've got an apartment, and the means to pay my mortgage and earn my own living. I've got security. Yes, I'd say I've got everything I need."

"Everything?" She didn't need to be looking at Will to know that his brows had lifted sardonically.

"What else would I need?"

"Let's say love, just for the sake of argument," he said drily. "Someone you love and who loves you. Someone to hold you and help you and make you laugh when you're down. Someone who can light up your world, and close it out when you're too tired to cope."

Someone like he had been, Alice thought involuntarily, and swallowed the sudden lump in her throat.

Dear Reader,

It was lovely to write this story in the middle of a gray English winter! St. Bonaventure is a fictional island, but it was inspired by various tropical beaches where I've sat in the raggedy shade of a coconut palm and looked out across a mint-green lagoon and been utterly happy.

Like my heroine, Alice, I spent quite a lot of my childhood overseas, and some of her memories are my own, but whereas I was left with an incurable case of itchy feet, Alice yearns for a settled, secure life. When she meets Will again, she is forced to choose how she wants her life to be. The safe option is to hold on to her past and stick with what she knows, but there *is* another option: to let go of the past and the mistakes she has made, and take a chance on loving and being loved completely. The risks are much greater—but then, so are the rewards.

Now Alice has to make her choice....

Best wishes,

Jessica

JESSICA HART

Barefoot Bride

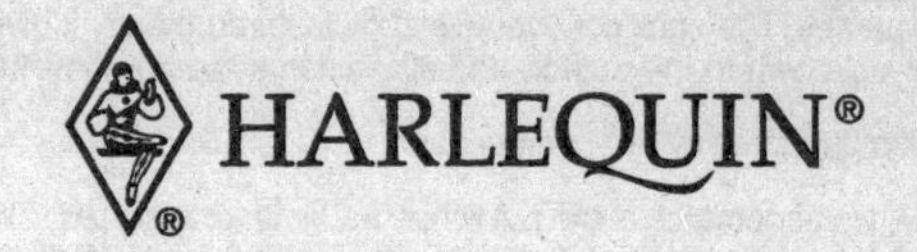

TORONTO • NEW YORK • LONDON
AMSTERDAM • PARIS • SYDNEY • HAMBURG
STOCKHOLM • ATHENS • TOKYO • MILAN • MADRID
PRAGUE • WARSAW • BUDAPEST • AUCKLAND

ISBN-13: 978-0-373-03939-5
ISBN-10: 0-373-03939-5

BAREFOOT BRIDE

First North American Publication 2007.

This edition published by arrangement with Harlequin Books S.A.

www.eHarlequin.com

Printed in U.S.A.

Award-winning author **Jessica Hart** was born in West Africa, and has suffered from itchy feet ever since—traveling and working around the world in a wide variety of interesting but very lowly jobs, all of which have provided inspiration to draw from when it comes to the settings and plots of her stories. Now she lives a rather more settled existence in York, where she has been able to pursue her interest in history, although she still yearns sometimes for wider horizons. If you'd like to know more about Jessica, visit her Web site www.jessicahart.co.uk

"Jessica Hart is a marvel."
—*www.romantictimes.com*

Jessica Hart won the 2005 RITA® Award
for Best Traditional romance with
Christmas Eve Marriage

* * *

She also won the Romantic Novelists' Association
Romance Award in 2006 for *Contracted: Corporate Wife*

"*Contracted: Corporate Wife* is romantic fiction
at its finest! Do not miss this brilliant romance
written by one of Harlequin Romance's
brightest stars!
—*www.cataromance.com*

CHAPTER ONE

'GUESS who I bumped into in town?'

Beth bounced down the steps into the garden and plonked herself onto the lounger next to Alice.

Alice had spent a blissful morning by the pool, feeling the tension slowly unwinding as the tropical heat seeped into her bones, and guiltily enjoying some time on her own. There was a puppyish enthusiasm about Roger's wife that could be quite exhausting at times, and, ever since she had arrived two days ago, Alice had been conscious of how hard Beth was trying to distract her from the fact that Tony was getting married tomorrow.

No one could be kinder or sunnier-natured than Beth, though, and Alice would have been very fond of her even if she wasn't married to Roger. And this was, after all, Beth's pool that she had been lying beside all morning. A good guest would be opening her eyes and sitting up to take an interest in her hostess's morning.

On the other hand, Beth *had* told her to relax before she'd gone out. Alice had done as she was told, and was now so relaxed she honestly couldn't summon the energy to open her eyes, let alone care which of Beth's many acquaintances she had met in town.

'Umm… Elvis?' she suggested lazily, enjoying the faint stir of warm breeze that ruffled the parasol above her.

'No!' Beth tsk-tsked at Alice's failure to take her exciting news more seriously, but she was much too nice to take offence. 'Someone we know… At least, I think you know him,' she added, suddenly dubious. 'I'm pretty sure that you do, anyway.'

That meant it could be anybody. Beth was unfailingly sociable, and gathered lame ducks under her wing wherever she went. When Roger and Beth had lived in London, Alice had often been summoned to parties where Beth fondly imagined her disparate friends would all bond and find each other as interesting as she did.

Sadly, Alice was by nature as critical and prickly as Beth was sweet and kind. She settled herself more comfortably on her lounger, resting an arm over her eyes and resigning herself to one of her friend's breathless accounts of someone Alice had met for five minutes several years ago, and who she had most likely hoped never to see again.

'I give up,' she said.

At least she wouldn't have to pay much attention for the next few minutes. Beth's stories tended to be long, and were often so muddled that she would get lost in the middle of them. All Alice would be required to do was to interject an occasional 'Really?' or the odd 'Oh?' between encouraging murmurs. 'Who did you meet?' she asked dutifully.

It was the cue Beth had been waiting for.

'Will Paxman,' she said.

Alice's eyes snapped open. 'What?' she demanded, jerking upright. *'Who?'*

'Will Paxman,' Beth repeated obligingly. 'He was a friend of Roger's from university…Well, you must have known him, too, Alice,' she went on with an enquiring look.

'Yes,' said Alice in a hollow voice. 'Yes, I did.'

How strange. She had convinced herself that she'd forgotten Will, or at least succeeded in consigning him firmly to the past, but all it had taken was the sound of his name to conjure up his image in heart-twisting detail.

Will. Will with the quiet, serious face and the stern mouth, and the disconcertingly humorous grey eyes. Will, who had made her heart jump every time he'd smiled his unexpected smile. He had asked her to marry him three times, and three times she had said no.

Alice had spent years telling herself that she had done the right thing.

She felt very odd. The last four years had been consumed by Tony, and she'd been braced for memories of him, not Will. Ever since Tony had left, she had done her best to armour herself against the pain of if onlys and what might have beens, to convince herself that she had moved on, only to be ambushed now by the past from quite a different direction.

Alice was totally unprepared to think about Will. She had thought that relationship was long over, and that she was safe from those memories at least, but now all Beth had to do was say his name and Alice was swamped by the old turbulence, uncertainty and bitter-sweetness of that time.

Beth was chatting on, oblivious to Alice's discomposure. 'I didn't recognize him straight away, but there was something really familiar about him. I've only met him a couple of times, and the last time was at our wedding, so that's...how long?'

'Eight years,' said Alice, carefully expressionless.

Eight years since Will had kissed her one last, fierce time. Eight years since he had asked her to marry him. Eight years since he had turned and walked away out of her life.

'It's hard to believe Roger has put up with me for that long!' Beth smiled, but Alice had seen the faint shadow cross her eyes and knew that her friend was thinking of the years she had spent trying to conceive. She and Roger had been open about their plans to start a family as soon as they were married, but it hadn't worked out that way. And, although they were unfailingly cheerful in company, Alice knew the sadness they both felt at their inability to have the children they wanted so much.

'Where did you meet Will?' she asked, wanting to distract Beth.

'In the supermarket, of all places!' Alice was pleased to see Beth's expression lighten as she swung her legs up onto the lounger and settled herself into a more comfortable position to recount her story. 'Isn't that an *amazing* coincidence? I mean, bumping into someone in a supermarket isn't that unusual, I know, but a supermarket in *St Bonaventure*? What are the odds of us all ending up on a tiny island in the Indian Ocean at the same time?'

'Will *is* a marine ecologist,' Alice felt obliged to point out. 'I guess the Indian Ocean isn't that odd a place to find him. It's more of a coincidence that Roger's been posted here. Not many bankers get to work on tropical islands.'

'No, we're so lucky,' Beth agreed happily. 'It's like being sent to Paradise for two years! And, now you're here, and Will's here, it's not even as if we've had to leave all our friends behind.'

She beamed at Alice, who immediately wondered if Beth was hatching a plan for a cosy foursome. It was the kind of thing Beth would do. It was Beth who had suggested that Alice come out for an extended visit while Tony was getting married.

'There are lots of single men out here,' she had told Alice. 'They won't be able to believe their luck when you turn up! A few weeks of uncritical adoration, and you won't care about Tony any more!'

Alice had no fault to find with this programme in principle, but not with Will. He knew her too well to adore her, and the last thing she wanted was Beth taking him aside and telling him how 'poor Alice's' world had fallen apart. He might be persuaded to take pity on her, and pretend he didn't remember how she had boasted of the great life she was going to have without him.

She would have to squash any matchmaking ideas Beth might have right now.

'I'm only here for six weeks,' she reminded Beth. 'And Will's probably just on holiday too. I don't suppose either of us will want to waste our precious holiday on politely catching-up on old times,' she added rather crushingly.

'Oh, Will's not on holiday,' said Beth. 'He's working here on some long-term environmental project. Something to do with the reef, I think.'

'But you'd have met him already if he'd been working here,' Alice objected. 'St Bonaventure is such a tiny place, you must know everybody!'

'We do, but Will's only been here a week, he said. I got the impression that he knows the island quite well, and that he's been here on various short trips, probably before Roger and I came out. But this is the first time he's brought his family with him, so I imagine they're going to settle here for a while.'

Alice's stomach performed an elaborate somersault and landed with a resounding splat, leaving her with a sick feeling that horrified her. 'Will's got a *family*?' she asked in involuntary dismay. She sat up and swung her feet to the warm tiles so that she could stare at Beth. 'Are you sure?'

Beth nodded, obviously surprised at Alice's reaction. 'He had his little girl with him. She was very cute.'

Will had a daughter. Alice struggled to assimilate the idea of him as a father, as a husband.

Why was she so surprised? Surely—*surely*, Alice—you

didn't expect him to stay loyal to your memory, did you? she asked herself.

Why on earth would he? She had refused him. End of story. Of *course* he would have moved on and made a life of his own, just as she had done. It wasn't as if she had been missing *him* all these years. She hadn't given him a thought when she'd been with Tony. Well, not very often, anyway. Only now and then, when she was feeling a bit low. If things had worked out, she would have been married by now herself.

Would that have made the news less of a shock? Alice wondered with characteristic honesty.

She could see that Beth was watching her curiously, and she struggled to assume an expression of unconcern. So much for her fears about Beth's matchmaking plans!

'I didn't know that he had married,' Alice said, hoping that she sounded mildly surprised rather than devastated, which was what she inexplicably felt. 'What was his wife like?'

'I didn't meet her,' Beth admitted. 'But I asked them to your welcome party tomorrow, and he said they'd like to come, so I guess we'll see her then.'

'Oh.' The sick feeling got abruptly worse. Somehow it seemed hard enough to adjust to the mere idea of Will being married, without having to actually face him and smile at the sight of him playing happy families, Alice thought bitterly, and then chided herself for being so mean-spirited.

She ought to be glad that Will had found happiness. She *was*, Alice told herself.

She was just a bit sorry for herself, too. None of the great plans she had made for herself had worked out. How confidently she had told Will that her life would be a success, that she wanted more than he could offer her. Alice cringed now at the memory. She wouldn't have much success to show off tomorrow. No marriage, no child, not even a job, let alone a good one.

Will, on the other hand, apparently had it all. He probably hadn't even been thinking about her all those years when the thought of how much he had loved her had been somehow comforting. It was all very…dispiriting.

'It's not a problem, is it?' asked Beth, who had been watching Alice's face rather more closely than Alice would have liked. Beth might be sweet and kind, but that didn't mean that she was stupid.

'No, no…of course not,' said Alice quickly. 'Of *course* not,' she added, although she wasn't entirely sure whether she was trying to convince herself or Beth.

How could it be a problem, after all? She and Will had split up by mutual agreement ten years ago, and she hadn't seen him for eight. There was no bitterness, no betrayal to mar their memories of the time they had spent together. There was absolutely no reason why they shouldn't meet now as friends.

Except—*be honest, Alice*—that he was married and she wasn't.

'Honestly,' she told Beth. 'I'm fine about it. In fact, it will be good to catch up with him again. It was just funny hearing about him suddenly after so long.'

She even managed a little laugh, but Beth was still looking sceptical, and Alice decided that she had better come clean. Roger was bound to tell his wife the truth anyway, and, if she didn't mention how close she and Will had been, Beth would wonder why she hadn't told her herself, and that would give the impression that she *did* have a problem with seeing Will again.

Which she didn't. Not really.

Slipping her feet into the gaudily decorated flip-flops she had bought at the airport at great expense, Alice bent to adjust one of the straps and let her straight brown hair swing forward to cover her face.

'You know, Will and I went out for a while,' she said as casually as she could.

'No!' Beth's jaw dropped. 'You and Will?' she said, suitably astounded. 'Roger never told me that!' she added accusingly.

'We'd split up long before he met you.' Alice gave a would-be careless shrug. 'It was old news by then. Roger probably never gave it a thought.'

'But you were both at our wedding,' Beth remembered. 'I do think Roger might have mentioned it in case I put you on the same table or something. I had no idea!' She leant forward. 'Wasn't it awkward?'

Unable to spend any more time fiddling with her shoe, Alice groped around beneath her lounger for the hair clip she had put there earlier.

'It was fine,' she said, making a big thing of shaking back her hair and twisting it carelessly up to secure it with the clip, all of which gave her the perfect excuse to avoid Beth's eye.

Because it hadn't been fine at all. There would have been no way she'd have missed Roger's wedding, and she had known that Will would be there. It had been two years since they had split up, and Alice had hoped that the two of them would be able to meet as friends.

It had been a short-lived hope. Alice had been aware of him from the moment she'd walked into the church and saw the back of his head. Her heart had jerked uncomfortably at the sight of him, and she had felt ridiculously glad that he was wedged into a pew between friends so that she wouldn't have to sit next to him straight away.

She had been going out with someone from work then. Clive, his name had been. And, yes, maybe he *had* been a bit of a stuffed shirt, but there had been no call for Will to talk about him that way. They had met, inevitably, at the reception after the service, and Alice had done her best to keep up a flow of increasingly desperate chit-chat as Will had eyed Clive and made absolutely no attempt to hide his contempt.

'You've sold out, Alice,' he told her later. 'Clive is boring, pretentious and self-obsessed, and that's putting it kindly! He's not the man for you.'

They argued, Alice remembered, in the hotel grounds, away from the lights and the music, as the reception wore on into the night. Clive had too much to drink, and to Alice's embarrassment was holding forth about his car and his clients and his bonuses. Depressed at her lack of judgement when it came to men, she slipped away, but, if she had known that she would encounter Will out in the dark gardens, she would have stuck with Clive showing off.

Will was the last person she wanted to witness Clive at his worst. She had been hoping to convince him that her life had been one long, upward curve since they had agreed to go their separate ways and that she was happily settled with a satisfying career, a stable home and a fulfilling relationship. No chance of him thinking that, when he had endured Clive's boasting all evening.

Mortified by Clive's behaviour, and tense from a day trying not to let Will realise just how aware she was of him still, Alice was in no mood for him to put her own thoughts into such brutal words.

'What do you know about it?' she fired back, glad of the dim light that hid her flush.

'I know you, and I know there's no way on earth a man like Clive could ever make you happy,' said Will, so infuriatingly calm that Alice's temper flared.

'You didn't make me happy, either!' she snapped, but Will just shook his head, unfazed by her lie.

'I did once,' he said. 'We made each other happy.'

Alice didn't want to remember those times. She turned her head away. 'That was then and this is now,' she said.

'We haven't changed.'

'*I* have,' Alice insisted. 'It's been nearly two years, Will. I'm not the same person I was before. I've got a new life, the life I always wanted.' She lifted her chin. 'Maybe Clive gives me what I need now.'

'Does he?' Will took a step towards her, and instinctively Alice backed away until she found herself up against a tree.

'Does he?' Will asked again softly, taking her by the wrists and lifting her arms until she was pinned against the tree trunk. 'Does he make you laugh, Alice? Do you lie in bed with him and talk and talk?' he went on, in the same low voice that reverberated up and down Alice's spine. 'The way you did with me?'

Her heart was thumping and she could feel the rough bark digging into her back through the flimsy material of her dress. She tried to pull her wrists away, but Will held her in place with insulting ease. He wasn't a particularly big man, but his spareness was deceptive, and his hands were much stronger than they looked.

And Alice, too, was conscious that she wasn't fighting as hard as she could have done. She could feel her treacherous body responding to Will's nearness. It had always been like that. Alice had used to lie awake sometimes, watching him while he slept, and wondering what it was about him that created such a powerful attraction.

It wasn't as if he were especially good-looking. In many ways, he was quite ordinary, but there was something about him, something uniquely Will in the line of his jaw, in the set of his mouth and the feel of his hands, in all the lean, lovely planes and angles of him that made her senses tingle still.

Will's voice dropped even further as he pressed her back against the tree. 'Do you shiver when he kisses you here?' he asked, dropping a light kiss on Alice's bare shoulder where it curved into her throat, and in spite of herself Alice felt that familiar shudder of excitement spiral slowly down to the very centre of her, where it throbbed and ached with memories of all the times they had made love.

Closing her eyes, she sucked in her breath as Will pressed warm, slow kisses up the side of her throat. 'That's none of your business,' she managed unsteadily.

'Does he love you?' Will whispered against her skin, and the brush of his lips made her shiver again.

She swallowed hard, her eyes still squeezed shut. 'Yes,' she said, but she knew it was a feeble effort. 'Yes, he does,' she tried again, although it sounded as if she was trying to convince herself.

Alice wanted to believe that Clive loved her, otherwise what was she doing with him?

'No, he doesn't,' said Will, and, although she couldn't see him, she knew that he was shaking his head. 'Clive doesn't love anybody but himself.'

There was a long pause, then Alice opened her eyes and found herself staring up into Will's face, the face that had once made her heart clench with the knowledge that she could touch it and kiss it and feel it whenever she wanted.

'Do you love Clive, Alice?' Will asked quietly.

Alice couldn't answer. Her throat was so tight it was hard enough to breathe, and all she could do was stand there, her arms pinioned above her head, and look back at him while the world stopped turning, and there was only Will and the feel of his hands over her wrists.

To her horror, her eyes filled with tears, and Will bent with a muffled curse to kiss her, a fierce, hard kiss that seared Alice to the soul. Nearly two years since they had said goodbye, but her mouth remembered his instantly, and she found herself kissing him back, angrily, hungrily, until Will released her wrists at last and yanked her into him to kiss her again.

Instinctively Alice's arms reached round him and she spread her hands over his back. It had been so long since she had held him, so long since she had felt the solidity and the hardness of the body she had once known as well as her own. She had forgotten how much she missed the feel of him and the wonderfully warm, clean, masculine scent of his skin.

'I've missed you,' Will echoed her thoughts in a ragged voice. 'I don't want to miss you again.'

'Will…' Alice was reeling, shocked by the emotion surging between them and the power of her own response.

'I'm going to Belize next week to work on the reef,' he went on, taking her face between his hands. 'Come with me,' he said with an urgency she had never heard from him before. 'Come with me and marry me, Alice. We need each other, you know we do. Clive has got his big, fat bonuses to keep him warm. He won't even notice you're gone. Say you'll come with me, and we can spend the rest of our lives making each other happy.'

And the truth was, Alice remembered by Beth's pool in St Bonaventure, that for a moment there she hesitated. Every fibre of her body was clamouring to throw herself back into his arms and agree.

And every cell in her brain was clanging a great, big warning.

She had the security she had yearned for at last. She had a good job, and in a year or two she would be in a position to get a mortgage and buy her own flat. Wasn't that what she had always wanted? A place of her own, where she could hang up her clothes in a wardrobe and never have to pack them up again? She was safe and settled. Did she really want to give that up to chase off to the Caribbean with Will, no matter how good it felt to kiss him again?

'Say yes,' Will urged her, encouraged by her hesitation.

Very slowly, Alice shook her head. 'No,' she said.

She would never forget the expression on his face then. Alice felt as if she had struck him.

'Why not?' he asked numbly.

'It wouldn't work, Will.' Alice pulled herself together with an effort. 'We went through all this two years ago. We agreed that we're different and we want different things. Our lives were going in different directions then, and they still are now. What's the point of pretending that they're not?'

'What's the point of pretending that what we have doesn't exist?' he countered, and she swallowed.

'It's just sexual chemistry,' she told him shakily. 'It's not enough.'

'And Clive and his bonuses are, I suppose?' Will made no attempt to hide the bitterness in his voice.

Alice didn't—couldn't—answer. It wasn't Clive, she wanted to tell him. It was the way her life seemed finally under control. She was settled, and had the kind of reassuring routine that she had craved when she was growing up.

And, yes, maybe Clive and the other boyfriends she had had weren't kindred spirits the way Will had been, but at least she knew where she was with them. They didn't make her entrails churn with excitement the way he had done, it was true, but they didn't make her feel superficial and materialistic for wanting to root herself with tangible assets either. Will was like her parents. He wanted things like freedom, adventure and independence, but Alice had learnt that you couldn't count on those. You couldn't put them in the bank and save them for when you needed them. Freedom, adventure and independence might be great things to have, but they didn't make you feel safe.

So all she did was look helplessly back at Will until he

dropped his hands, his expression closed. 'That's three times I've asked you to marry me,' he said bleakly as Alice lowered her trembling arms and rubbed them unsteadily. 'And three times you've said no. I've got the message now, though,' he told her. 'I won't ask you again.'

He had stepped away from her then, only turning back almost against his will for one last, hard kiss. 'Goodbye, Alice,' he said, and then he turned and walked out of her life.

Until now.

Alice sighed. For a while there, the past had seemed more vivid than the present, and her heart was like a cold fist in her chest, just as it had been then.

'Are you sure?' asked Beth, whose blue eyes could be uncomfortably shrewd at times.

'Of course.' Alice summoned a bright smile. 'It was fine,' she repeated, knowing that Beth was afraid that tension between her and Will would mar the party she had planned so carefully. 'And it will be fine this time, too. Don't worry, Beth. I promise you I don't have a problem meeting Will or his wife,' she went on bravely, if inaccurately, as she got to her feet. 'Will probably won't even remember me. Now, why don't I give you a hand unpacking all that shopping?'

Will watched anxiously as Lily took Beth's hand after a moment's hesitation and allowed herself to be led off to the pool, which was already full of children squealing excitedly. His daughter had looked apprehensive at the thought of making new friends, but she hadn't clung to him or even looked to him for reassurance. He was almost as much a stranger to her as Beth was, he reflected bitterly.

'She'll be fine.' Roger misread Will's tension. 'Beth loves kids, and she'll look after Lily. By the time the party's over, she won't want to go home!'

That was precisely what Will was afraid of, but he didn't want to burden Roger with his problems the moment that they met up again after so long. He'd always liked Roger, and Beth's delight at bumping into him the day before had been touching, but the truth was that he wasn't in the mood for a party.

He hadn't been able to think of a tactful way to refuse Beth's invitation at the time, and this morning he had convinced himself that a party would be a good thing for Lily, no matter how little he might feel like it himself. Beth had assured him that it would be a casual barbecue, and that several families would be there, so Lily would have plenty of other children to play with.

Will hadn't seen his daughter play once since they had arrived in St Bonaventure, and he knew he needed to make an effort to get her to interact with other children. But, watching Lily trail reluctantly along in Beth's wake, Will was seized by a fresh sense of inadequacy. Should he have reassured her, or gone with her? He was bitterly aware that he was thrown by the kind of everyday situations any normal father would take in his stride.

'Come and have a beer,' said Roger, before Will could decide whether to follow Lily and Beth or not, so he let Roger hand him a bottle so cold that the condensation steamed. There wasn't much he could do about Lily right now, and in the meantime he had better exert himself to be sociable.

The two men spent a few minutes catching up and, by the time Roger offered to introduce him to the other guests, Will was beginning to relax. He didn't know whether it was the beer, or Roger's friendly ordinariness, but he was definitely feeling better.

'Most people are outside,' said Roger, leading the way through a bright, modern living-area to where sliding-glass doors separated the air-conditioned coolness from the tropical heat outside.

Will was happy to follow him. He had never minded the heat, and, if he was outside, he'd be able to keep an eye on Lily at the pool. Roger glanced out as he pulled open the door for Will, then hesitated at the last moment.

'Beth did tell you who's staying with us, didn't she?' he asked, suddenly doubtful.

'No, who's that?' asked Will without much interest as he stepped out onto the decking, shaded by a pergola covered in scrambling pink bougainvillaea.

He never heard Roger's answer.

He saw her in his first casual glance out at the garden, and his heart slammed to a halt in his chest.

Alice.

She was standing in the middle of the manicured lawn, talking to a portly man in a florid shirt. Eight years, and he recognized her instantly.

Even from a distance, Will could see that her companion was sweating profusely in the heat, but Alice looked cool and elegant in a loose, pale green dress that wafted slightly in the hot breeze. She was wearing high-heeled sandals with delicate straps, and her hair was clipped up in a way that would look messy on most other women, but which she carried off with that flair she had always had.

Alice. There was no one else like her.

He had thought he would never see her again. Will's heart stuttered into life after that first, jarring moment of sheer disbelief, but he was still having trouble breathing. Buffeted by a turbulent mixture of shock, joy, anger and something perilously close to panic, Will wasn't sure what he felt, other than totally unprepared for the sight of her.

Dimly, Will was aware that Roger was saying something,

but he couldn't hear it. He could just stare at Alice across the garden until, as if sensing his stunned gaze, she turned her head, and her smile froze at the sight of him.

There was a long, long pause when it seemed to Will as if the squawking birds and the shrieking children and the buzz of conversation all faded into a silence broken only by the erratic thump of his heart. He couldn't have moved if he had tried.

Then he saw Alice make an excuse to the man in the ghastly shirt and turn to walk across the garden towards him, apparently quite at ease in those ridiculous shoes, the dress floating around her legs.

She had always moved with a straight-backed, unconscious grace that had fascinated Will, and as he watched her he had the vertiginous feeling that time had ground to a halt and was rewinding faster and faster through the blur of the last ten years. So strong was the sensation that he was half-convinced that, by the time she reached him those long years would have vanished and they would both be back as they had been then, when they'd loved each other.

Will's mouth was dry as Alice hesitated for a fraction of a second at the bottom of the steps that led up to the decking, and then she was standing before him.

'Hello, Will,' she said.

CHAPTER TWO

'ALICE.' Will's throat was so constricted that her name was all he could manage.

Roger looked from one to the other, and took the easy way out. 'I'd better make sure everyone has a drink,' he said, although neither of them gave any sign that they had even heard him. 'I'll leave you two to catch up.'

Will stared at Alice, hardly able to believe that she was actually standing in front of him. His first stunned thought was that she hadn't changed at all. There were the same high cheekbones, the same golden eyes and slanting brows, the same wide mouth. The silky brown hair was even pulled carelessly away from her face just the way she had used to wear it as a student. She was the same!

But when he looked more closely, the illusion faded. She must be thirty-two now, ten years older than the way he remembered her, and it showed in the faint lines and the drawn look around her eyes. Her hairstyle might not have changed, but the quirky collection of dangly, ethnic earrings had been replaced by discreet pearl studs, and the comfortable boots by high heels and glamour.

Alice had never been beautiful. Her hair was too straight, her features too irregular, but she had possessed an innate stylishness and charm that had clearly matured into elegance and sophistication. She had become a poised, attractive woman.

But she wasn't the Alice he had loved. That Alice had been a vivid, astringent presence, prickly and insecure at times—but who wasn't, when they were young? When she'd talked, her whole body had become animated, and she would lean forward and gesticulate, her small hands swooping and darting in the air to emphasise her point, making the bangles she wore chink and jingle, or shaking her head so that her earrings swung wildly and caught the light.

Will had loved just to watch the way the expressions had chased themselves across her transparent face. It had always been easy to tell what Alice had been feeling. No one could look crosser than Alice when she was angry; no one else's face lit like hers when she was happy. And when she was amused, she would throw back her head and laugh that uninhibited, unexpectedly dirty laugh, the mere memory of which was enough to make his groin tighten.

Ironically, the very things that Will had treasured about her had been the things Alice was desperate to change. She hadn't wanted to be unconventional. She hadn't wanted to be different. She'd wanted to be like everyone else.

And now it looked as if she had got her wish. All that fire, all that quirkiness, all that personality…all gone. Firmly suppressed and locked away until she was as bland as the rest of the world.

It made Will very sad to realise that the Alice who had haunted him all these years didn't exist any more. In her place was just a smart, rather tense woman with unusual-coloured eyes and inappropriate shoes.

'How are you, Alice?' he managed after a moment.

Alice's feet were killing her, and her heart was thumping and thudding so painfully in her chest that it was making her feel quite sick, but she produced a brilliant smile.

'I'm fine,' she told him. 'Great, in fact. And you?'

'I'm OK,' said Will, who was, in fact, feeling very strange. He had been pitched from shock to joy to bitter disappointment in the space of little more than a minute, and he was finding it hard to keep up with the rapid change of emotions.

'Quite a surprise bumping into you here,' Alice persevered in the same brittle style, and he eyed her with dismay. When had the fiery, intent Alice learnt to do meaningless chit-chat? She was treating him as if he were some slight acquaintance, not a man she had lived with and laughed with and loved with.

'Yes,' he agreed slowly, thinking that 'surprise' wasn't quite the word for it. 'Beth didn't tell me that you were here.'

'I don't think she made any connection between us,' said Alice carelessly. 'It wouldn't have occurred to Beth to mention me to you. She didn't know that we'd been…'

'Lovers?' suggested Will with a sardonic look when she trailed off.

A slight flush rose in Alice's cheeks. 'I didn't put it quite like that,' she said repressively. 'I just said that we had been close when we were students together.'

'It's not like you to be coy, Alice.'

She looked at him sharply. 'What do you mean?'

'You and Roger were *close*,' said Will. 'You and I were in love.'

Alice's eyes slid away from his. She didn't want to be reminded of how much she had loved him. She certainly didn't want a discussion of how in love they had been. No way could she cope with that right now.

'Whatever,' she said as carelessly as she could. 'Beth got the point, anyway.'

He had changed, she thought, unaccountably disconsolate. Of course, she had known in her head that he wasn't going to be the same. Ten years, marriage and children were bound to have had an effect on him.

But in her heart she had imagined him still the Will she had known. The Will she had loved.

This Will seemed taller than she remembered, taller and tougher. His neck had thickened slightly and his chest had filled out, and the air of calm competence she had always associated with him had solidified. He still had those big, capable hands, but there was none of the amusement she remembered in his face, no familiar ironic gleam in the grey eyes. Instead, there were lines around his eyes and deeper grooves carved on either side of his mouth, which was set in a new, hard line.

It was strange, talking to someone at once so familiar and so much a stranger. Meeting Will like that was even worse than Alice had expected. She had planned to be friendly to him, charming to his wife and engaging to his child, so that they would all go away convinced that she had no regrets and without the slightest idea that her life wasn't quite the glittering success she had so confidently expected it to be.

She might as well have spared herself the effort, Alice thought ruefully. In spite of all her careful preparations, her confidence had evaporated the moment she'd laid eyes on him, and she was as shaken and jittery as if Will had turned up without a moment's warning. She knew that she was coming over as brittle, but she couldn't seem to do anything about it.

'Beth said that you were working out here,' she said, opting to stick with her social manner, no matter how uncomfortable it felt. It was easier than looking into his eyes and asking him if he had missed her at all, if he had wondered, as she had done, whether life would have been different if she had said yes instead of no that day.

Will nodded, apparently willing to follow her lead and stick to polite superficialities. 'I'm coordinating a major project on sustainable tourism,' he said, and Alice raised her brows.

'You're not a marine ecologist any more?' she asked, surprised. Will had always been so passionate about the ocean, she couldn't imagine him giving up diving in favour of paperwork.

'I am, of course,' he corrected her. 'But I don't do straight research anymore. A lot of our work is assessing the environmental impact of major development projects on the sea.'

Alice frowned. 'What's that got to do with tourism?'

'Tourism has a huge effect on the environment,' said Will. 'The economy here desperately needs the income tourists can bring, but tourists won't come unless there's an international airport, roads, hotels, restaurants and leisure facilities...all of which use up precious natural resources and add to the weight of pollution, which in turn affects the delicate balance of the environment.'

Will gestured around him. 'St Bonaventure is a paradise in lots of ways. It's everyone's idea of a tropical island, and it's still unspoilt. Its reef is one of the great undiscovered diving spots in the world. That makes it the kind of place tourists want to visit, but they won't come all this way if the development ends up destroying the very things that makes this place so special.

'The government here needs to balance their need to get the money to improve the living standards of the people here with the risk to the reef,' he went on. 'If the reef is damaged, it will not only destroy the potential revenue from tourism, it'll also leave the island itself at risk. The reef is the most effective protection St Bonaventure has against the power of the ocean.'

Will stopped, hearing himself in lecture mode. The old Alice might have been interested, but this one certainly wasn't. Instead of leaning forward intently and asking awkward questions, the way she would have done before, she wore an expression of interest that was little more than polite.

'Anyway, the project I'm coordinating is about balancing the needs of the reef with the needs of the economy before tourism is developed to any great extent,' he finished lamely.

'Sounds important,' Alice commented.

He glanced at her, as if suspecting mockery. 'It is,' he said.

Alice had deliberately kept her voice light to disguise the pang inside. For a moment there he had been the Will she remembered, his face alight with enthusiasm, his eyes warm with commitment.

What would it be like to work on something you believed in, something that really mattered, not just to you but to other people as well? Alice wondered. When it boiled down to it, her own career in market research was just about making money. It hadn't changed any lives other than her own.

That had never bothered her before, but she had had to question a lot of things about her life in the last year. What did her much-vaunted career amount to now, after all? Nothing, thought Alice bleakly.

Will had built his career on his expertise and his passion. He had done what he wanted the way he'd wanted to do it. He had found someone to share his life and had fathered a child. His life since Roger's wedding had been successful by any measure, while hers… Well, better not go there, Alice decided with an inward sigh.

'What about you?' Will asked, breaking into her thoughts and making her start.

'Me?'

'What are you doing on St Bonaventure?'

Alice wished she could say that she was here for some interesting or meaningful reason. 'I'm on holiday,' she confessed, immediately feeling guilty about it.

'So you'll just be here a couple of weeks?'

She was sure she detected relief in his voice. He was

probably delighted at the idea that she wouldn't be around for long so that he could get on with his happy, successful, *married* life without her.

The thought stiffened Alice's resolve not to let Will so much as guess that all her careful plans had come to nothing. It wasn't that she begrudged him his happiness, but a girl had her pride. She needed to convince him that she had never had a moment's regret. She wouldn't lie—that would be pathetic, obviously—but there was no reason why she shouldn't put a positive slant on things, was there?

'Actually,' she said, 'I'm here for six weeks.'

He lifted one brow in a way that Alice had often longed to be able to do. 'Long holiday,' he commented.

'I'm lucky, aren't I?' she agreed with a cool smile. 'Roger and Beth have been telling me I should come and visit ever since they were posted here last year, but I just haven't had the opportunity until now.'

Redundancy could be seen as an opportunity, couldn't it?

'You must have done well for yourself,' said Will. 'Not many people get the opportunity for a six-week holiday.'

'It's not strictly a holiday,' Alice conceded. 'As it happens, I'm between jobs at the moment,' she explained, tilting her chin slightly.

That wasn't a lie, either. She might not have another job lined up just yet, but when she went home she was determined that she was not only going to get her career back on track, but that she would be moving onto to bigger and better things. With her experience, there was no reason why she shouldn't aim for a more prestigious company, a promotion *and* a pay raise.

'I see,' said Will, his expression so non-committal that Alice was afraid that he saw only too well. He had no doubt interpreted being 'between jobs' as unemployed, which of course was another way of looking at it, but not one Alice was prepared to dwell on.

'I was in a very pressurised work environment,' she told him loftily. 'And I thought it was time to take a break and reassess where my career was going.'

Strictly speaking, of course, it had been the company who had taken over PLMR who had decided that Alice could have all the time she wanted to think about things, but Will didn't need to know that. It wasn't as if it had been her fault. Almost all her colleagues had been made redundant at the same time, she reminded herself. It could happen to anyone these days.

'Market research—it *is* market research, isn't it?—obviously pays well if you can afford six weeks somewhere like this when you're between jobs,' said Will, with just a hint of snideness. 'But then, you always wanted to make money, didn't you?'

'I wanted to be secure,' said Alice, hating the faintly defensive note in her voice. 'And I am.' What was wrong with wanting security? 'I wanted to be successful, and I am,' she added for good measure.

Well, she had been until last year, but, when your company was the subject of a hostile takeover, there wasn't much you could do about it, no matter how good you were at your job.

It hadn't been a good year. Her only lucky break had been winning nearly two thousand pounds in the lottery, and that had been a fluke. Normally, Alice wouldn't even have thought about buying a ticket, but she had been in a mood when she was prepared to try anything to change the dreary trend of her life.

It wasn't as if she had won millions. Two thousand pounds wasn't enough to change her life, but it was just enough for a ticket to an out-of-the-way place like St Bonaventure, and Alice had taken it as a sign. At any other time, she would have been sensible. She would have bought herself a pair of shoes and put the rest of the money towards some much-needed repairs on her flat—the unexpected windfall would have covered the cost of a new boiler, for instance—but that hadn't been any other time. That had been the day she heard that Tony and Sandi were getting married.

Alice had gone straight out and bought a plane ticket. *And* some shoes.

Still, there was no harm in letting Will think that she had earned so much money that she didn't know what to do with it all. Not that it would impress him. He was more likely to disapprove of what he thought of as her materialistic lifestyle, but Alice was desperate for him to believe that she had made it.

'We all make choices,' she reminded him. 'I made mine, and I don't have any regrets,'

'I'm glad you got what you wanted, then,' said Will flatly.

'You too,' said Alice, and for a jarring moment their eyes met. It was as if the polite mask they both wore dropped for an instant, and they saw each other properly for the first time. The sense of recognition was like a blow to Alice's stomach, pushing the air from her lungs and leaving her breathless and giddy and almost nauseous.

But then Will jerked his head away, the guarded expression clanging back into place with such finality that Alice wondered if she had imagined that look.

'You didn't marry Clive, then?' he asked abruptly.

'Clive?' Alice was thrown by the sudden change of subject.

'The Clive you were so in love with at Roger and Beth's wedding,' Will reminded her with an edge of savagery. 'Don't tell me you've forgotten him!'

'I didn't—' Alice opened her mouth to strenuously deny ever loving Clive and then shut it again. If she hadn't loved Clive, why had she let Will believe that she did? Why hadn't she been able to tell him the truth that day?

'No, I didn't marry Clive,' she said quietly. 'We split up soon after…after Roger's wedding,' she finished after a tiny moment of hesitation.

She had so nearly said 'after you kissed me', and she might as well have done. The memory of that dark night in the hotel gardens jangled in the air between them. Those desperate kisses, the spiralling excitement, the sense of utter rightness at being back in each other's arms.

The tightness around her heart as she'd watched him walk away.

Alice could feel them all as vividly as if they had kissed the night before.

Will had to be remembering those kisses too. She wanted to be able to talk about it, laugh about it even, pretend that it didn't matter and it was all in the past, but she couldn't. Not yet.

So she drew a steadying breath and summoned another of her bright smiles. 'Then I met Tony, and we were together for four years. We talked about getting married, but…well, we decided it wouldn't have worked.'

Tony had decided that, anyway.

'We stopped ourselves making a terrible mistake just in time,' Alice finished.

OK, it might not be the whole story, but why should she tell Will all her sad secrets? Anyway, it might not be the *whole* truth, but it *was* the truth. It *would* have been a mistake if she and Tony had gone ahead with the wedding. Nothing but unhappiness would have come from their marriage when Tony was in love with someone else. Alice's world might have fallen apart the day Tony had sat her down to tell her about Sandi, but she'd accepted even then that he had done the right thing.

Today was Tony and Sandi's wedding day, Alice was startled to remember. She had spent so long dreading this day, imagining how hard it would be for her to think about another woman taking what should have been her place, and, now that it was here, she hadn't even thought about it.

Perhaps she ought to be grateful to Will for distracting her?

Will drained the last of his beer and turned aside to put the empty bottle on the decking rail. 'Still avoiding commitment, I see,' he commented with a sardonic glance over his shoulder at Alice, who flushed at the injustice of it.

She wasn't the one who had called off the wedding. If it had been down to her, she would be happily married to Tony right now, but she bit back the words. She had just convinced him that ending her engagement to Tony had been a mutual decision, so she could hardly tell him the truth now.

Which was worse? That he thought she was afraid of commitment, or that he felt sorry for her?

No question.

'Still determined not to get married until I'm absolutely sure it's perfect,' she corrected Will. 'So...I'm fancy free, and on the lookout for Mr Right. I'm not going to get married until I've found him, and, until then I'm just having fun!'

Will was unimpressed by her bravado. 'You seem very tense for someone who's having fun,' he said.

Alice gritted her teeth. 'I am *not* tense,' she snapped. Tensely, in fact. 'I'm a bit jet-lagged, that's all. I only got here a couple of days ago.'

'Ah,' said Will, not bothering to hide the fact that he was totally unconvinced by her explanation. Which just made Alice even crosser, but she sucked in her breath and resisted the temptation to retort in kind. She didn't want Will to think that he was getting to her, or that she cared in the slightest what he thought of her.

Friendly but unobtainable, wasn't that how she wanted him to think of her? Pleasant but cool. His long-lost love who had turned into a mysterious stranger. Anything but sad and tense and a failure.

She fixed a smile to her face. 'I gather you weren't as hesitant about taking the plunge,' she said.

'The plunge?'

'Marriage,' she reminded him sweetly, and a strange expression flitted over his face.

'Ah. Yes. I did get married,' he agreed. 'Why? Did you think I would never get over you?'

'Of course not,' said Alice with dignity. 'If I thought about you at all—which I can't say was that often—' she added crushingly, 'it was only to hope that you were happy.'

Will raised his brows in disbelief. 'Really?'

'Yes, really.' Alice had been nursing a glass of Roger's lethal tropical punch, but it didn't seem to be having a very good effect on her. She set it on the rail next to Will's empty bottle.

'*Have* you been happy?' she asked him, the words out of her mouth before she had thought about them properly.

Will didn't answer immediately. He thought about Lily, about how it had felt when he had held his daughter in his arms for the first time. About drifting along the reef, fish flitting past him in flashes of iridescent colour and looking up to see the sunlight filtering down through the water to the deep blue silence. About sitting on a boat and watching dolphins curving and cresting in the foamy wake, while the water glittered and the sea breeze lifted his hair.

He had been happy then. It hadn't been the same feeling as the happiness he had felt lying next to Alice after they had made love, holding her into the curve of his body, smoothing his hand over her soft skin, breathing in her fragrance, marvelling that this quirky, contrary, vibrant woman was really his, but, still, he *had* been happy since.

In a different way, but, yes, he'd been happy.

'I've had times of great happiness,' he said eventually, very conscious of Alice's great golden eyes on his face. 'But not in my marriage,' he found himself admitting. 'We weren't as sensible as you. We didn't realise what a mistake we were making until it was too late.'

It had been his fault, really. He had vowed to move on after Roger's wedding, had been determined to put Alice from his mind once and for all. The trouble was that every woman he'd met had seemed dull and somehow colourless after Alice. They might have been prettier and nicer, and certainly sweeter, but, when he'd closed his eyes, it had always been Alice's blazing golden eyes that he saw, always Alice's voice that he heard, always Alice's skin that he tasted.

Nikki had been the first woman with the strength of personality to match Alice's, and Will had persuaded himself that she was capable of banishing Alice's ghost once and for all. They had married after a whirlwind holiday romance in the Red Sea where he had been researching at the time.

It had been madness to take such a step when they'd barely known each other. Will should have known that it would end in disaster. Because Nikki hadn't been Alice. She had been forceful rather than colourful, efficient rather than intense. The only thing the two women had shared, as far as Will could see, was a determination to make a success of themselves.

Nikki, it had turned out too late, had had no intention of wasting her life in the kind of countries where Will felt most at home. 'My career's at home,' she had told him. 'There's nothing for me to do here, nothing works, and, if you think I'm having the baby in that hospital, you've got another think coming!'

Lily was the result of a failed attempt to make the marriage work. She'd been born in London, just as Nikki had planned, but by then Nikki had already sued for divorce. 'It's never going to work, Will,' she'd told him when he came to see his new daughter. 'Let's just accept it now rather than waste any more time.'

'We were married less than two years,' he told Alice.

'So you're divorced?' she said, horrified at the instinctive lightening of her heart, and ashamed of herself for feeling even a smidgeon of relief that his life hadn't turned out quite as perfectly as it had seemed at first.

And that she wouldn't have to face his wife after all. Although she wished now that she hadn't said that about 'looking for Mr Right'. She didn't want Will thinking that she would try and pick up where they had left off the moment she realised that he was single.

'I'm sorry,' she said, when he nodded curtly. 'I didn't realise. Beth said that you had your family with you, so we just assumed that you were married.'

'No, it's just me and Lily,' he said. 'My daughter,' he added in explanation. 'She's six.'

'Is she spending the holiday with you?' Alice didn't have much to do with children, and was a bit vague about school terms, but she supposed mid-March might conceivably mean the Easter holidays. It seemed a bit early, though. Perhaps it didn't matter so much for six-year-olds?

'No, she lives with me,' said Will, almost reluctantly.

'Oh? That's unusual, isn't it?' Alice looked surprised. 'Doesn't the mother usually have custody?'

'Nikki did,' he said. 'She died recently, so now Lily only has me.'

'God, how awful!' Alice was shocked out of her cool pose, and Will was absurdly pleased to see the genuine compassion in her eyes. He had been wondering if there was anything left of the old Alice at all. 'What happened? Or maybe you don't want to talk about it?' she added contritely.

'No, it's OK. People are going to have to know, and obviously it's difficult to explain in front of Lily.' Will sighed. 'That's why I couldn't tell Beth when we met her in the supermarket. Lily is finding it hard enough to adjust without hearing the whole story talked over with perfect strangers.'

'I can imagine.'

'Lily used to go to the after-school club, and Nikki would pick her up after work. But that day there had apparently been some meeting that had run on, so she was going to be very late at the school. They'd warned her before about being late, so she was rushing to get there, and I suppose she wasn't driving as carefully as she should …'

'A car accident?' said Alice when he trailed off with a sigh.

'She was killed instantly, they said.' Will nodded, and Alice wondered just how much his ex-wife still meant to him. You could say that the marriage had been a mistake, but they had had a child together. He must have had some feelings still for Lily's mother.

'Meanwhile, Lily is still waiting for her mother to come and pick her up?' she said gently.

Will shot her a curious look, as if surprised by her understanding. 'I think she must be. She hasn't talked about it, and she's such a quiet little girl anyway, it's hard to know how much she understands.'

He looked so tired suddenly that Alice felt guilty for being so brittle and defensive earlier. 'It must have been a shock for you, too,' she said after a moment.

Will shrugged his own feelings aside. 'I was in Honduras when I heard. It took them some time to track me down, so I missed the immediate aftermath. I wasn't there for Lily,' he added, and, from the undercurrent of bitterness in his voice, Alice guessed he flayed himself with that knowledge.

'You weren't to know,' she said in a deliberately practical voice. 'What happened to Lily?'

'Nikki's parents live nearby so the school called them when she didn't turn up, and they looked after Lily until I got there. My work's kept me overseas for the last few years, though, and I haven't had the chance to see her very often, so I'm virtually a stranger to her.' Will ran his fingers through his hair in a gesture of defeat. 'To be honest, it's all been a bit...difficult.'

Difficult? Alice thought about his small daughter. Lily was six, he had said. What would it be like to have the centre of your world disappear without warning, and to be handed over instead to a father you hardly knew? Alice's heart was wrung. Her own parents had been dippy and unreliable in lots of ways, but at least they had always been there.

'When did all this happen?' she asked.

'Seven weeks ago.'

'Seven *weeks*? Is that all?' Alice looked at Will incredulously, her sympathy evaporating. 'What are you doing out here?'

Will narrowed his eyes at her tone. 'My job,' he said in a hard voice. 'I've already delayed the project by over a month.'

'You shouldn't be thinking about your *job,*' said Alice with a withering look. 'You should be thinking about your daughter!'

'I am thinking about her.' Will set his teeth and told himself he wasn't going to let Alice rile him. 'I'm hoping that the change of scene will help her.'

He couldn't have said anything more calculated to catch Alice on the raw. His casual assumption that a change of scene could only be good for a child reminded her all too painfully of the way her own parents had blithely uprooted her just when she had settled down in a new country and started to feel at home.

'We're off to Guyana,' they had announced gaily. 'You'll love it!'

After Guyana, they had spent a year on a croft in the Hebrides. 'It'll be good for you,' her father had decided. Then it had been Sri Lanka— 'Won't it be exciting?'—followed by Morocco, Indonesia, Exmoor (a disaster) and Goa, although Alice had lost track of the order they had come in.

'You're so lucky,' everyone had told her when she had been growing up. 'You've seen so much of the world and had such wonderful experiences.'

But Alice hadn't felt lucky. She hadn't wanted any more new experiences. She had longed to settle down and feel at home, instead of being continually overwhelmed by strange new sights and sounds, smells and people.

And she hadn't had the loss of a mother to deal with at the same time. Alice's heart went out to Will's daughter.

Poor Lily. Poor little girl.

CHAPTER THREE

'YOU don't think it would have helped her more to stay in familiar surroundings?' Alice asked Will sharply, too irritated by his apparent disregard for his daughter to think about the fact that it was probably none of her business.

A muscle was twitching in Will's jaw. 'Her grandparents offered to look after her,' he admitted. 'But they're getting on. Besides, we all thought that it would be easier for Lily to start a new life without continual painful reminders of her mother. She's going to have to get used to living with me some time, so it's better that she does that sooner rather than later.'

His careful arguments were just making Alice crosser. 'Why couldn't *you* get used to doing a job that meant you could stay where Lily would feel at home?' she demanded.

'There's not a lot of work for marine ecologists in London!'

'You could change your job.'

'And do what?' asked Will, stung by her tone, and annoyed with letting himself be drawn into an argument with Alice, who was typically holding forth on a subject she knew little about.

Her brittleness had vanished, and she was vivid once more, her cheeks flushed and her tawny eyes flashing as she waved her arms around to prove her point. Suddenly, she was the

Alice he remembered, and Will was simultaneously delighted and exasperated.

It was an uncannily familiar feeling, he thought, not knowing whether he wanted to shake her or catch her into his arms. The rush of joy he felt at realising that the real Alice was still there was tempered by resentment of her unerring ability to home in on the very issue he felt most guilty about. He wouldn't have minded if they'd been arguing about something unimportant, but this was his daughter they were discussing. Will was desperate to be a good father, and he didn't need Alice pointing out exactly where he was going wrong five minutes after meeting him again.

'Marine ecology is all I know,' he tried to explain. 'I have to support my child financially as well as emotionally, and the best way I can do that is by sticking with the career that I know rather than launching wildly into some new one where I'd have to start at the beginning. Besides,' he went on as Alice looked profoundly unconvinced. 'Lily isn't my only responsibility. This project has taken five years to set up, and a lot of futures depend on it being successful. Of course Lily is important, but I've got responsibilities to other people as well. That's just the way things are, and Lily's going to have to get used to it.'

'That's an incredibly selfish attitude,' said Alice, twirling her hand dramatically so that she could poke her finger towards Will's chest. 'It's all about what suits *you*, isn't it? All about what *you* need. What about what *Lily* needs?'

'I'm her father,' said Will tersely. 'Lily needs to be with me.'

'I'd agree with you, if being with you meant staying in a home she knew, with her grandparents and her friends and her routines.'

Alice knew that it wasn't really her business, but Will's complacency infuriated her. 'Losing a mother would be hard enough for her to deal with even if she had those things to hang on to, but you've dragged her across the world to a strange country, a place where she doesn't know anyone or anything, and by your own admission she doesn't even know you very well!'

She drew an impatient breath. 'Did you ever think of asking Lily what *she* wanted to do?'

'Lily's six.' Will bit out the words, too angry by now to care whether Alice knew how effectively she was winding him up. 'She's not old enough to make an informed decision about anything, let alone where she wants to live. She's just a little girl. How can she possibly judge what's best for her?'

'She's old enough to know where she feels comfortable and who she feels safe with,' Alice retorted.

Will gritted his teeth. Her comments were like a dentist drilling on a raw nerve. Did she really think he didn't feel guilty enough already about Lily? He hated the fact that he was practically a stranger to his own daughter. He *hated* the fact that Lily was lost and unhappy and he seemed powerless to help her. He was doing the best that he could, and, yes, maybe it wasn't good enough, but he didn't need Alice to point that out.

That brief surge of joy he had felt at her transformation from a brittle nonentity into the vibrant, fiery creature he remembered was submerged beneath a wave of resentment, and he eyed her with dislike.

'I thought you'd changed, Alice,' he said. 'But you haven't, have you?'

She tilted her chin at him in a characteristically combative gesture. 'What do you mean?'

'You still hold forth about subjects you know absolutely nothing about,' he said cuttingly. 'You know nothing about my daughter, nothing about the situation and nothing about me, now, but that doesn't stop you, does it?'

He gave a harsh laugh. 'You know, I used to think it was quite amusing the way you used to base your opinions on nothing more than instinct and emotion. For someone so obsessed with fitting things into neat categories, it always seemed odd that you refused to look at the evidence before you made up your mind. But I don't think it's very funny anymore,' he went on. 'It's pointless and narrow-minded. Perhaps, just once, you should try finding out the facts before you open your mouth and start spouting your personal prejudice!'

There was a stricken look in Alice's golden eyes but Will swept on, too angry to let himself notice and feel bad about it.

He was fed up. It had been a hellish seven weeks. He was worried sick about his daughter, and he had a daunting task ahead to get a complex but incredibly important project off the ground. The last thing he needed was the inevitable turmoil of dealing with Alice.

This was typical of her. Time and again over the last eight years, Will had told himself that he was over her. That he was getting on with his life. That he wouldn't want her even if he *did* meet her again. And then he would catch a glimpse of a straight back through a crowd, or hear a dirty laugh at a party, and his heart would jerk, and he would feel sick with disappointment to realise that it wasn't Alice after all.

And now—*now* when he had so much else to deal with—here she was, with characteristically perverse timing, threatening to turn his world upside down just when he least needed it!

Well, this time it wasn't going to turn upside down, Will determined. He had wasted the last ten years of his life getting over Alice, and he wasn't going to waste another ten minutes. It was just as well that they had come face to face, he decided. It had reminded him of all the things about her that had used to irritate him, and that made it so much easier to walk away this time.

'You know, I could stand here and pontificate to you if I could be bothered,' he told Alice, his words like a lash. 'I could tell you that you've thrown away everything that was warm and special about you, and turned yourself into someone brittle and superficial with dull earrings and silly shoes, but I won't because, unlike you, I don't believe in passing judgement on people I've only met for five minutes!'

Alice only just prevented herself from flinching at his tone. She had no intention of showing Will how hard his words had struck home. She managed an artificial laugh instead, knowing that she sounded just as brittle as he had accused her of being.

'You've got a short memory, if you think we've only known each other for five minutes!'

'You're not the Alice I knew,' said Will in the same, hard voice. 'I liked her. I don't like you. But that doesn't give me the right to tell you how to live your life, so don't tell me how to live mine. Now, if you'll excuse me, I'll go and find the daughter you seem to think I care so little about before you accuse me of neglect.'

And, with that, he turned and headed down the steps towards the pool, leaving Alice alone on the decking, white with fury mixed with a sickening sense of guilt. She shouldn't have said all that about his daughter. Will was right, she *didn't* know the situation, and she had probably been unfair. She had let the bottled-up resentment about her own childhood get the better of her. She should apologise.

But not yet.

I don't like you. Will's bitter words jangled in the air as if he had shouted them out loud. Alice felt ridiculously conspicuous, sure that everyone had heard and everyone was looking at her. They were probably all thinking that they didn't like her either, she thought miserably

Her throat was tight with tears that she refused to shed. She hadn't let anyone see her cry about Tony, so she certainly wasn't about to start blubbing over Will. She didn't care if he didn't like her. She didn't care what he thought. She didn't care about anything.

'You haven't got a drink, Alice.' Roger materialised beside her. 'Is everything OK?'

Roger. Alice nearly did cry then. Dear Roger, her dearest friend. The only one she could rely on through thick and thin.

She blinked fiercely. 'You like me, don't you, Roger?'

'Oh, you're all right, I suppose,' said Roger with mock nonchalance, but he put his arms round her and hugged her close. 'What's the matter?' he asked in a different tone.

'Nothing,' said Alice, muffled against his chest.

'Come on, it's just me. Was it seeing Will again?'

Alice drew a shuddering breath. 'He's changed,' she muttered.

'We've all changed,' said Roger gently.

'You haven't.' Shc lifted her head and looked up into his dear, familiar face. She had met Roger on her first day at university, and they had been best friends ever since. For Alice, he was the brother she had never had, and not Beth, not even Will, had come between them. 'That's why I love you,' she said with a wobbly smile.

Roger pretended to look alarmed. 'An open declaration of affection! This isn't like you, Alice. You *are* upset!'

'Only because Will was rude about my shoes,' said Alice, tilting her chin. 'They're not silly, are they, Roger?'

Straight-faced, Roger studied the delicate sandals, decorated with sequins and blue butterflies. 'They're fabulous,' he told her. 'Just like you. Now, come and have another drink before we both get maudlin and I tell you I love you too!'

'All right.' Alice took a deep breath and steadied her smile. 'But only if you introduce me to all these single men Beth promised me,' she said, determined to put Will Paxman right out of her mind. 'And not that guy in the awful shirt with the perspiration problem,' she added, following Roger into the kitchen.

'Colin,' said Roger, nodding knowledgeably as he handed her another glass of punch. 'No, we'll see if we can do better for you than that!'

He was as good as his word, and Alice soon found herself the centre of a circle of admiring men, all much more attractive and entertaining than the hapless Colin. Alice was under no illusions about her own looks, but she appreciated that, living in a small expatriate community with a limited social life, these men would be interested in any single, available female, and she did her best to sparkle and live up to the reputation Beth had evidently created for her. But it was hard when all the time she was aware of Will's dark, glowering presence over by the pool.

Alice turned her back pointedly, but it didn't make much difference. She could practically feel his cold grey eyes boring into her spine, and the thought made her shiver slightly and take a gulp of her punch.

Why was he bothering to watch her, anyway? There were no shortage of women simpering up at him by the pool, all of them wearing shoes and lipstick and apparently indulging in small talk. Alice was prepared to concede that she might be wrong, but none of them gave the impression of being intellectual giants. How come Will didn't find *them* prickly and false?

Defiantly, Alice emptied her glass and let someone whose name she had already forgotten rush off to get her a refill. If Will thought her brittle and superficial, superficial and brittle she would be!

Flirting was not something that came naturally to her but it was amazing what she could do when glacial grey eyes were watching her with open disapproval. What right had Will Paxman to disapprove of her, anyway? She was just being sociable, which was more than he was doing, and she was damned if she was going to skulk away to the kitchen just because he didn't like her.

So she smiled and laughed and made great play with her eyelashes while she shifted her weight surreptitiously from foot to foot to try and relieve the pressure from her shoes, which might look fabulous but which were, in truth, becoming increasingly uncomfortable. Not that Alice would ever have admitted as much to Will.

The tropical sun combined with Roger's punch was giving her a thumping headache, and Alice's bright smile grew more and more fixed as she concentrated on being fun and ignoring Will. Still, she was doing all right until someone mentioned honeymoons and suddenly she remembered that today was Tony's wedding day.

All at once Alice's bottled-up misery burst through its dam and hit her with such force that she only just managed to stop herself doubling over as if from a blow. The pain and anger and humiliation she had felt when Tony had left her for Sandi was mixed up now with a nauseating concoction of shock, regret, guilt and hurt at Will's reaction to meeting her again after all this time.

Not to mention an excess of Roger's punch.

Unable to keep up the façade any longer, Alice murmured an excuse about finding a hat and headed blindly for the house. At least there it would be cool.

And full of people. She hesitated at the bottom of the steps leading up to the decking. The large, airy living area would be packed with people enjoying the air conditioning and someone would be bound to see her sneak off to her room. The next thing Beth would be there, knocking on the door, wanting to know what was wrong.

Changing her mind, Alice glanced over her shoulder to

make sure that Will wasn't watching her, and realised that she couldn't see him. All that time she had spent simultaneously ignoring him and trying to convince him that she was having the best time of her life, and he hadn't even been there!

Humiliation closed around her throat like a fist. She had been so sure that he was watching her—he *had* been at first!—and now the idea that he had got bored and gone off while she'd been still desperately performing for his benefit made her feel an idiot. No, worse than an idiot. *Pathetic*.

Close to tears, Alice slipped unnoticed along the side of the house and ducked beneath an arch laden with a magnificent display of bougainvillaea that divided the perfectly manicured front garden from a shady and scrubby patch of ground at the back behind the kitchen and servants' quarters.

Beth had a maid to help with the housework, a smiling woman called Chantelle, and this was her domain. There were wooden steps leading down from the kitchen verandah where she would sit sometimes, her fingers busy with some mindless task while she sang quietly to herself. Alice wouldn't normally have intruded, but Chantelle, she knew, was busy clearing up after the barbecue lunch, and Alice didn't think she would mind if she sat there for a little while on her own.

The garden here was blissfully shady and overgrown, so dark that Alice was almost at the steps before she realised that she was not the only person needing some time alone. A little girl was sitting on the bottom step, half-hidden in the shadow of a banana tree. Her knees were drawn up to her chin, and she hugged them to her, keeping very still as she watched a butterfly with improbably large iridescent blue wings come to rest on her shoe.

Alice stopped as soon as she saw them, but the butterfly had already taken off and was flapping languidly in and out of the patches of sunlight. The child spotted her at the same time, and she seemed to freeze. Alice was reminded of a small, wary animal trying to make up its mind whether to bolt for cover or not.

She was sorry that she had interrupted, but it seemed rude to turn on her heel and walk off without saying anything. Besides, there was something very familiar about the scene. Alice couldn't work out what it was at first, but then she realised that the little girl reminded her of herself as a lonely, uncertain child.

'I'm sorry, I didn't mean to disturb you, or the butterfly. I was just looking for somewhere quiet to sit for a while.' She paused, but the little girl just looked guardedly at her, still poised for flight.

She wasn't a particularly pretty child. She had straight, shapeless hair and a pinched little face dominated by a pair of huge, solemn dark eyes. Her expression was distrustful, but Alice was conscious of a pang of fellow feeling.

How many times had she slipped off to find a place to hide while she'd waited for her parents to take her back to wherever they were calling home at the time? This child's parents were probably having a great time by the pool, totally oblivious to the fact that their daughter had slipped away, intimidated by the other children who were noisy and boisterous and seemed to be able to make friends without even trying.

'I wanted to escape from the party for a bit,' Alice explained. 'It's too noisy and I didn't know anyone to talk to properly. Is that what you did?' she asked as the girl glanced sharply at her.

The child nodded.

'The thing is, I don't want to go back yet,' said Alice. 'And I can't think of anywhere else to hide. Do you mind if I sit next to you, just for a little while? I won't talk if you don't want to. I hate it when people talk to me when I'm trying to be quiet.'

There was a flash of recognition in the girl's watchful eyes, and, while she didn't exactly agree, she didn't say no either, and as Alice went over she shifted along the step to make room for her. Encouraged, Alice settled next to her, drawing her knees up to mirror the child's posture.

A strangely companionable silence settled round them. In the distance, Alice could hear the buzz of party conversation, punctuated by the occasional burst of laughter, and the squeals and shrieks and splashes from the pool, but they seemed to be coming from a long way away, far from the dark, drowsy green world of the kitchen garden where there was only the squawk of a passing raucous bird and the low-level hum of insects to break the hot quiet.

She was glad of the chance to settle her nerves. Meeting Will again had left her jangled and distressed, and it was hard to disentangle her feelings about him from all the hurt and confusion she had felt since Tony had left. Between them, they had left her feeling utterly wretched.

If only she could rewind time and do things differently, this afternoon at least, Alice thought miserably. Seeing Will hadn't been at all the way she had imagined. *He* wasn't the man she had imagined him to be. If she had become brittle and superficial, he had grown hard and bitter. The young man with the humorous eyes and the reassuring steadiness had gone for good. Now that she knew what he had become, she couldn't even dream of him the way he had been.

The realisation that the Will she had loved was lost for ever felt like a bereavement. Alice's throat worked, and she pressed her lips hard together to stop herself crying.

There was no point in this, she told herself. She was upset because it was Tony's wedding day, but that was no excuse. She had behaved badly. She had been defensive and unsympathetic and rude. No wonder Will hadn't liked her. Now he had obviously left the party without saying goodbye, and she might not have another chance to say that she was sorry.

It was no use trying to tell herself that she didn't care. Here in the quiet garden with her restful companion she could acknowledge that she did.

'There's the butterfly again.' The little girl broke the silence in hushed tones, and they both sat very still as the butterfly alighted on an upturned bucket. It was so big that it seemed almost clumsy, its wings so heavy that it blundered from perch to perch, flapping slowly through the hot air as if barely able to keep itself aloft.

The child's eyes were huge as she watched it. 'I've never seen such a big butterfly before!'

She obviously hadn't been on the island that long, Alice reflected, although she could probably have told that anyway from her pale skin.

'When I was a little girl I lived in Guyana,' Alice said. 'That's in South America, and it was hot and humid, like this. Our house was on the edge of the jungle, and the garden was full of butterflies—blue ones and green ones and yellow ones, and butterflies with stripes and spots and weird patterns. Some of them were enormous.'

'Bigger than that one?'

'Much bigger.' Alice spread out her fingers to demonstrate the wing span. 'Like this.'

The girl's eyes widened further as she looked from the butterfly to Alice's hand and back again, clearly trying to imagine a garden full of such creatures.

'It must have been pretty,' she commented.

'They were beautiful,' Alice remembered almost in surprise. Funny, she hadn't thought about the garden in Guyana for years. 'I used to sit on the verandah steps, just like we're doing now, and watch them for hours.'

The little girl looked solemn. 'Didn't you have any friends?'

'Not then,' said Alice. 'It was very isolated where we lived, and I didn't know many other children. I used to pretend that the butterflies were my friends.'

How odd to remember that now, after all these years! She smiled, not unkindly, at her younger self.

'I imagined that they were fairies in disguise,' she confided to her small companion. It was strange how she felt more comfortable sitting here with the child than she had in the thick of a party thrown especially for her. Alice had never been a particularly maternal type, but she felt a strong sense of affinity with this quiet, plain little girl with her dark, wary eyes.

'Fairies?' the child breathed, riveted.

'At night I thought their beautiful wings would turn into silk robes and gorgeously coloured dresses.' Somehow it didn't sound silly in this dark, tropical garden. 'You know the sound the insects make when it's dark here?'

The girl nodded but her mouth turned down slightly. 'I don't like it. It's loud.'

'It was loud in Guyana, too,' said Alice. 'I used to think it was frightening, and then my father told me one night that it was just the sound of all the insects having a great party!'

Her father had been good at nonsense like that. He'd told the young Alice extravagant stories, embellishing them until they were more and more absurd, and she had struggled to know how much to believe. She ought to remember the good times more often, Alice thought with a sudden pang. It wasn't often that she thought of her childhood with affection, but it hadn't been all bad.

'So after that, whenever I couldn't sleep because it was too hot, I'd lie there listening to the noise and imagine the butterflies talking and laughing and dancing all night.'

She laughed softly, but the little girl looked struck. 'I was a bit frightened by the noise too,' she confessed. 'But now I'll think about them having a party like you said, and it won't seem so strange.'

'You'll soon get used to it,' Alice reassured her, and then nudged her, pointing silently as the butterfly came lumbering through the air towards them again. They both held their breath as it came closer and closer, fluttering indecisively for what seemed like ages before it settled at last on Alice's foot.

The child's eyes widened in delight as she noticed for the first time that Alice's shoes were decorated with tiny fabric butterflies, their beads and sequins catching the light, and she put a hand to her mouth to smother a giggle.

'He likes your shoes,' she whispered. 'Do you think he knows those butterflies aren't real?'

Alice considered. 'I'm not sure. Probably not. He doesn't look like a very clever butterfly, does he?'

A laugh escaped through the rather grubby little fingers, rousing the butterfly to flight once more, but Alice didn't mind. It was such a pleasure to see the small, serious face lighten with a real smile. She guessed it didn't happen very often and her heart constricted with a kind of pity. A little girl like this should be laughing and smiling all the time.

'I like your shoes,' she said to Alice, who stretched out her legs so that they could both admire them.

'*I* like them too,' she agreed. 'But somebody told me today that they were silly.' Her face darkened as she remembered Will's comment.

'I don't think they're stupid. I think they're really nice.'

'Well, thank you.' Alice was ridiculously heartened by her approval. She peered down at the small feet next to her. 'What are yours like?'

'They're just shoes,' the child said without enthusiasm.

Alice could see what she meant. She was wearing sturdy

leather sandals which were perfectly practical but lacked any sense of fun or fashion.

'When I was little I wanted a pair of pink shoes,' she said sympathetically. 'I asked my parents for years, but I never got them.'

'I'd like pink shoes too, but my dad says these are more sensible.' The little girl sighed.

'Dads don't understand about shoes,' Alice told her. 'Very few men do. But, when you grow up, you'll be able to buy any shoes you want. I bought a pair of lovely pink shoes as soon as I was earning my own money. Now I've got lots of shoes in different colours. Some of them are lots of fun. I've got shoes with polka dots and zebra stripes,' she said, illustrating the patterns by drawing in the air. 'Some of them have got sequins, or bows, or fancy jewels or—'

'Jewels?' she interrupted, starry-eyed. 'Real ones?'

'Well, no, not *exactly*,' Alice had to admit. 'But they look fabulous!'

The child heaved an envious sigh. 'I wish I could see them.'

Alice opened her mouth to offer a view of the collection she had brought with her, but before she could ask the little girl her name a voice behind them made them both jump.

'Lily?'

Will stepped out of the kitchen onto the wooden verandah, letting the screen door bang into place behind him. He had been looking for his daughter everywhere.

Unable to bear the sight of Alice flirting any longer, he had been avoiding the front lawn, and had endured instead a tedious half-hour making small talk in the air-conditioned coolness of the living room. Only when he'd thought that he could reasonably make an excuse and leave had he realised that Lily was not among the children around the pool where he had left her.

Since then he had been searching with rising panic, flaying

himself for ever taking his eyes off her in the first place, and now acute relief at finding her safe sharpened his voice.

'What do you think you're—'

He stopped abruptly as he reached the edge of the verandah and saw who was sitting at the bottom of the steps next to his daughter, both of them staring up at him with identically startled expressions.

'Alice!'

Will glared accusingly at her. If Alice hadn't annoyed him so much, he wouldn't have left the poolside, and he would have kept a closer eye on Lily. This was all her fault.

'What are *you* doing here?' he asked rudely. It was bad enough when he had imagined her out front, making a spectacle of herself with all those fawning men, but it was somehow worse to find her here with Lily, a witness to his inadequacies as a father.

Why did it have to be *her*? He wouldn't have minded finding anyone else with Lily, would even have been glad that his daughter had found a friend, but not Alice. She had been free enough with her opinion of him as a father earlier. There would be no stopping her now that she had met Lily. Alice would have taken one look at his quiet, withdrawn daughter and decided just how he was failing her, Will thought bleakly.

CHAPTER FOUR

ALICE took her time getting to her feet. Slowly brushing down the back of her dress, she wondered how best to deal with him. She didn't want to argue in front of Lily—how stupid of her not to have guessed who she was, but she didn't look anything like Will—but it was obvious that Will was still angry with her.

Obvious too that he hadn't liked finding her with his daughter. She just hoped he wouldn't think that she had done it deliberately.

'We were just talking about shoes,' she said carefully at last. 'We hadn't got round to introducing ourselves, had we?' she said to Lily, who had turned away from her father and was sitting hunched up, her fine hair swinging down to hide her face.

Lily shook her head mutely. With the appearance of her father, she had lost all her animation.

'I'm Alice,' said Alice, persevering. 'And you're...Lily? Is that right?'

Lily managed a nod, but she peeped a glance under her hair at Alice, who smiled encouragingly.

'Nice to meet you, Lily. Shall we shake hands? That's what people do when they meet each other for the first time.'

It felt like a huge victory when Lily held out her hand, and Alice shook it with determined cheerfulness. She wished she could tell Will to stop looming over his daughter. He looked so forbidding, no wonder Lily was subdued.

'What are you doing out here, Lily?' Will asked stiffly. 'Don't you want to play with the other children in the pool?'

Lily's face was closed. 'I like talking to Alice,' she said, without turning to look at him.

There was an uncomfortable silence. Alice looked from Will to his daughter and back again. He had told her that he was practically a stranger to his own child, but she hadn't appreciated until now just what that meant for the two of them. Will was awkward and uncertain, and Lily a solitary child still trying to come to terms with the loss of her mother. Neither knew how to make the connection they both needed so badly.

It wasn't her business. Will wanted her to leave him alone with his daughter, that much was clear. She should just walk away and let them sort it out themselves.

But when Alice looked at Lily's hunched shoulders, and remembered how she had laughed at the butterfly, she couldn't do it. Will didn't have to accept her help, but his little girl needed a friend.

'I liked talking to you, too,' she said to Lily. 'Maybe we can meet again?' She glanced at Will, trusting that he wouldn't jump on the offer before Lily had a chance to say what she wanted. 'Do you think your dad would let you come round to tea one day?'

'Can I see your shoes?' asked Lily, glancing up from under her hair.

'You can see some of them,' said Alice. 'I'm only here on holiday, so I didn't bring them all with me, but I've got some fun ones. The others are at home in London.'

Lily thought for a moment and then looked over her shoulder at her father. 'Can I?'

Most other little girls would have been jumping up and

down, swinging on their daddy's hand and cajoling him with smiles and dimples, supremely confident of their power to wrap their fathers round their perfect little fingers, but not Lily. She would ask his permission, but she wouldn't give him smiles and affection. Not yet, anyway.

A muscle worked in Will's jaw. He wished that he knew how to reach her. He knew how sad she was, how lost and lonely she must feel. If only he could find some way to break down the barrier she had erected around herself.

Torn, he watched her stiff back helplessly. He wanted to give Lily whatever she wanted, but Alice and her shoes and her talk about London would only remind her of her mother and her life in England, and she would be unsettled all over again. Surely that was the last thing she needed right now?

He was still hesitating when Beth burst through the screen door with her customary exuberance. 'Will?' she called. 'Are you out here? Did you—' She stopped as she caught sight of the three of them. 'Oh, good, you've found her—and Alice too!'

Belatedly sensing a certain tension in the air, she looked from one to the other. 'I'm not interrupting anything, am I?'

'Of course not.' Alice forced a smile. 'I was just inviting Lily round for tea one day.'

'What a lovely idea!' Beth clapped her hands together and beamed at Will. 'Come tomorrow!'

Will could feel himself being swept along by the force of her enthusiasm and tried to dig in his heels before it all got out of hand. 'I'm sure you'll have had enough visitors by then,' he temporised while he thought up a better excuse.

'Nonsense,' said Beth briskly. 'I've hardly had a chance to talk to anyone today. You know what it's like at a party. You're always saying hello or goodbye or making sure everyone's got a drink. It would be lovely to see you and Lily tomorrow. Otherwise it'll all feel like an awful anticlimax, and we'll get scratchy with each other. At least, if you come, Roger and Alice will have to behave.' She laughed merrily. 'It's not as if you'll be working on a Sunday, is it?'

'No,' Will had to admit.

'And Lily needs to make friends for when you're not there,' Beth reminded him.

'I've brought a nanny out from England,' said Will, irritated by the implication that he hadn't given any thought to child-care arrangements. What did they think? That he was planning to go off to work and leave Lily alone in the house every day?

'Oh, you should have brought her along today.' Beth was blithely unaware of his exasperation, but Alice was keeping a carefully neutral expression, Will noticed. She would know exactly how he was feeling.

'It's her day off,' he said, forcing a more pleasant note into his voice. It wasn't Beth's fault that Alice was able to unsettle him just by standing there and saying nothing. 'She wanted to go snorkelling.'

'Well, bring her tomorrow,' Beth instructed. 'Then she'll know where we are, and she and Lily can come again when you're at work.'

Will glanced back at Lily. She had lifted her head and was watching the adults talking. Her face was brighter than he had seen it, he thought, and his heart twisted.

I like talking to Alice, she had said. He couldn't refuse her just because he remembered talking to Alice himself. And what would be the harm, after all? He didn't have to have anything to do with Alice. He could just have tea and then let Dee take over the social side of things.

'All right,' he succumbed, and was rewarded by a flash of something close to gratitude in Lily's eyes. 'Thank you, we'd like to come.'

* * *

Alice disliked Dee, Lily's nanny, on sight. What had Will been thinking of, hiring someone quite so young and silly to look after his daughter? Or had he been thinking more about what a pretty girl she was? How long her legs were, how sparkling her blue eyes, how soft the blonde hair she tossed back from her face as she giggled?

Lily was subdued, and Will positively morose, but Dee made up for both of them with her inane chatter—and he had called *her* superficial! Alice listened in disbelief as Dee rambled on about her family and her friends, and what a good time she had had learning how to snorkel the day before.

As far as Alice could tell, she had absolutely nothing in common with Will or Lily. It was hard to imagine anyone less suited to dealing with a quiet, withdrawn child, she thought disapprovingly. Still, if Dec's particular brand of silliness was what Will wanted to come home to in the evening, that was his business. She was only thinking about Lily.

Unable to bear Dee's inanities any longer, Alice leant over to Lily. 'Would you like to come and see my shoes?' she whispered as Dee talked on, and Lily nodded. She took the hand Alice held out quite willingly and trotted beside her to the bedroom, where a selection of Alice's favourite shoes had been spread out on the bed.

'Which ones do you like best?' Alice asked, after Lily had examined them all seriously.

After much thought, Lily selected pair of black high heels with peep toes and floppy bows covered in polka dots.

'Good choice,' said Alice approvingly. 'They're my favourites too. Why don't you try them on?' she added, and watched as Lily slipped her small feet into the shoes and turned to look at herself in the mirror.

'Wait!' Alice rummaged in a drawer and pulled out a diaphanous sarong. Tying it round the little girl, she draped some pearls over her and added her favourite straw hat with its wide brim. 'There!'

She stood back to admire the effect, delighted by the look on Lily's face as she studied her reflection. The sullen expression was gone and, animated, the piquant face looked positively pretty beneath the hat.

Will would like to see her like this, Alice thought. 'Let's show the others,' she suggested casually.

Biting her lip as she concentrated on her balance, Lily teetered down the corridor. 'May I introduce Miss Lily Paxman?' Alice announced grandly as she flung open the door.

There was a chorus of oohs and aahs, and a broad smile spread across Lily's face. Alice happened to glance at Will just then, and the expression in his eyes as he watched his daughter smile brought a lump to her throat. She would never be able to accuse Will of not caring about Lily now.

Feeling as if she had intruded on a very private moment, she looked away and caught Roger's eye.

'OK?' he mouthed.

Alice nodded and went over to stand next to him, leaving Beth and Dee exclaiming over Lily. Dee, in particular, was going completely over the top with her compliments. Probably trying to impress Will, Alice thought sourly. Too bad Dee didn't know that Will didn't go in for gushing sentimentality.

At least, he never used to. He had changed so much that for all Alice knew sweet, fluffy women were just his type nowadays. He certainly didn't have much time for sharp, astringent ones, that was for sure.

Without quite being aware of it, Alice sighed.

'What's the matter?' asked Roger.

'Oh...nothing.'

Not wanting to look at Will, Alice watched Beth instead.

'She's fantastic with kids, isn't she?' she said, and Roger's smile twisted as his eyes rested on his wife.

'She loves children.'

Roger and Beth had never talked much about their inability to conceive, but Alice knew how much having a baby would mean to both of them. She tucked her hand through Roger's arm and leant against him, offering wordless comfort. 'It must be hard for her at times like this,' she said quietly. 'For you, too.'

'It's just that you can't help imagining what it would be like if it was your own child dressing up …' Roger trailed off, and Alice hugged his arm closer in silent sympathy. He and Beth were both so easy-going and good-humoured that it was easy to forget that they had their own problems to deal with.

On the other side of the room, Will watched Alice standing close to Roger and frowned. Only a moment ago he had been feeling grateful to her. Lily's smile might not have been meant just for him, but still it had warmed his heart, and it was down to Alice, he knew. She had been able to connect with his daughter in a way that eluded him.

But, when he looked at her to try and indicate his gratitude somehow, he saw that she wasn't even aware of Lily any more. Instead she was leaning against Roger, her arm tucked through his and her head on his shoulder. It was a very intimate pose.

Too intimate for a man whose wife was only a few feet away.

Will glanced at Beth, who was smiling at Lily as she adjusted her hat. She seemed unaware of Roger and Alice over by the window, but Will had noticed a fleeting expression of sadness in her face more than once now, and he wondered how much Beth knew, or guessed, about her husband's feelings for Alice.

It was a long time since he and Roger had shared that drunken evening, but Will had never forgotten the look in Roger's eyes as he confessed the truth. He couldn't remember where Alice had been, but Roger had just split up with yet another girlfriend, and Will had been deputed to help him drown his sorrows and provide a shoulder to cry on.

'I don't want him to be alone,' Alice had said. She'd always been very protective of Roger, which was ironic in its own way, Will reflected.

It had been very late and very dark when Will had helped a reeling Roger home at last. He had never known if Roger had meant to tell him that all the other girls were just an attempt to disguise how he felt about Alice, or if the next day he had even remembered the truth he had blurted out. Neither of them had ever mentioned it again, but Will couldn't shake the memory of the bleakness in Roger's face.

'I'm just her friend,' he had said, slurring his words. 'I'll only ever be her friend.'

Had Roger decided to settle for second best with Beth? Will hoped not. He liked Roger's wife. She deserved better than that.

What was Alice doing, snuggled up to Roger like that? Will scowled. Did she know how Roger felt about her? Had she guessed?

'I'm looking for Mr Right,' she had told him with that bright, brittle smile he hated. Easy to see how Roger might fill that role for her. He was kind, loyal, funny, the rock Alice had fallen back on more than once. It wouldn't be hard to imagine the scales falling from her eyes as friendship turned to love…

But Alice wouldn't do that to Beth, would she? Will's frown deepened. The old Alice would never do anything to hurt her friends, but what did he know of her now? The old Alice wouldn't have stood that close to Roger, either.

She would have been standing close to *him*, leaning against him, touching him.

Will pushed the thought aside and got abruptly to his feet. 'It think it's time we went,' he said.

'What did you think of Dee?' Beth asked Alice when Will had chivvied a disappointed Lily and Dee out to the car.

'Not much,' said Alice, unimpressed. She felt oddly disgruntled. It wasn't that she had wanted to see Will, but he could have stayed a bit longer instead of rushing them off like that. It wasn't very fair on Lily. 'She tries too hard. You can tell she's desperate to impress Will.'

Beth looked at her strangely. 'You can?'

'Well, it's a classic, isn't it?' Alice sniffed. 'Child, nanny, single father...alone together on a tropical island... Of *course* she's going to fall for him!'

'It's interesting you should say that,' said Beth. 'I wouldn't have said that she was the slightest bit interested in Will. He's too old for her.'

'Old?' repeated Alice, outraged. 'He's not *old*! He's only thirty-five!'

'I expect that seems old to Dee,' said Beth, choosing not to comment on how well Alice remembered Will's age. 'She can't be much more than twenty. I'd say she was much more impressed by that hunk who taught her how to snorkel yesterday. Didn't you hear her going on about him?'

'No.' Alice frowned. She wasn't as openly friendly as Beth, and had frankly tuned out most of Dee's prattling. She wasn't quite ready to believe that Dee had no interest in Will, either. He might be a bit older, but Dee could hardly have failed to notice that he was an attractive man—any more than Will would have missed the fact that she was young and very pretty. One could accuse Will of being lots of things, but unobservant wasn't one of them.

'I don't know how Will could possibly have thought she would make a suitable nanny,' she said crossly.

Beth laughed. 'Nannies aren't buxom old ladies in mob caps any more, you know! Dee is young and friendly and enthusiastic. I expect Will thought she would be fun for Lily to have around.'

'Or fun for *him* to have around?' suggested Alice, her voice laced with vinegar. 'You're not going to tell me he didn't clock those long legs and that body when he interviewed her?'

'She's certainly a very pretty girl,' Beth agreed equably. 'But it wasn't Dee he was watching today, and it wasn't Dee he couldn't take his eyes off yesterday.'

Alice, who had prowling restlessly around the room, stopped and stared at Beth, who smiled blandly back.

'I don't think you need to worry about Dee,' she said.

'I'm not worried about Dee,' snapped Alice, severely ruffled. 'Will can do what he likes. *I* don't care. We don't even like each other any more.'

'Ah.' Beth nodded understandingly. 'Right. That'll be why you both spent the entire time watching each other when you thought the other one wasn't looking.' She paused. 'I think there's still a real connection between you.'

Alice flushed. 'There's no connection,' she insisted. 'Not any more.'

And there wasn't, she reminded herself repeatedly over the next few days. Will had hardly spoken to her at the tea, and she certainly hadn't been aware of him watching her. Whenever she'd happened to glance at him—and it wasn't that often, no matter what Beth had said—he'd seemed intent on talking to Roger or Beth, or watching Lily and Dee. If he'd even noticed that *she* was in the room, he'd hidden it extremely well, she thought grouchily.

There certainly hadn't been any opportunity for her to tell him that she was sorry for her tactless comments at the party.

Not that Will would care whether she apologised or not. He had made it very clear how he felt about her now. Beth's idea of a connection between them was ludicrous, Alice thought more than once over the next week, refusing each time to consider why the realisation should make her feel so bleak. Any sense of connectedness that had once existed between her and Will had been broken long ago, and there was no hope of repairing it now.

And she wouldn't want to, even if it had been possible, Alice reminded herself firmly. She hadn't been lying when she had told Will that this time in St Bonaventure was her chance to think about what she really wanted out of life. Redundancy and Tony's rejection had brought her to a crossroads, and, if the last miserable few months had taught her anything, it was that she needed to look forward, not back.

There was no point in hankering after the past or what had been. Of all the options that lay open to her now, the one route she wouldn't take was the one she had already travelled. She had to make her own future, and that certainly didn't include resurrecting old relationships that had been doomed in the first place.

No, she was going to have a good time while she was here, Alice decided, and then she was going to go home and rebuild her life so that it was bigger and better than before. She would get herself a really good job. She might even sell her flat, and make a fresh start somewhere new where memories weren't lurking behind every door, waiting to ambush her when her resistance was low.

And she would do it all by herself. She wasn't going to rely on anyone else to make her happy this time. The only way to be sure was to do it alone.

In spite of all her resolutions, Alice found her mind wandering to Will uncomfortably often over the next few days. Having been catapulted back into her life without warning, Will had disappeared again so completely, it left Alice feeling mildly disorientated.

Had that really been Will standing there, after all these

years? Sometimes she wondered if she had dreamt the entire episode, but she knew that she hadn't made up Lily. That guarded little face with the clouded dark eyes were all too vivid in her memory. Alice hoped that she was adjusting to her new life and learning to trust Will. She kept thinking about the look in his eyes when he had seen his daughter smiling, and every time it brought a lump to her throat.

She would have liked to be able to help them understand each other, but then she would remind herself that they didn't need her help. They had Dee, and no doubt they were already well on the way to being a happy little family.

Alice imagined Will going home every night to Dee, who would already know how he liked his tea—strong and black. By now she would know that he hated eggs, and his gestures would be becoming familiar to her. She would recognize how he rubbed his hand over his face when he was tired, how amusement would light the grey eyes and lift the corner of his mouth.

Oh, yes, Lily and Will would be fine without Alice. They didn't need her when they had Dee.

Which left her free to enjoy her holiday.

She should have been delighted at the prospect, but instead Alice felt scratchy and increasingly restless as the days passed. She had longed and longed for a few weeks doing absolutely nothing in the sunshine, but the truth was that she was getting a bit bored of sitting by the pool all day.

Beth had a full social agenda, and Alice was included in all the invitations, but there were only so many coffee mornings and lunches at the club that she could take. All that gossip and moaning about maids, school fees, how hard it was to get bacon or a decent gin and tonic! Beth was so open and friendly that she was welcome anywhere, but Alice knew that her own brand of acerbity went down rather less well.

In spite of having grown up overseas, she had never come

across the expat lifestyle like this before. Her parents would never have dreamed of joining a club with other expatriates. They didn't care about air-conditioning or supermarkets, and chose to live in remote tribal villages where they could be 'close to the people', a phrase that still made Alice nearly as uncomfortable as a lunch with some of Beth's fellow wives.

Why was it she never seemed to fit in anywhere? Alice wondered glumly. All she had ever wanted was to belong somewhere, but the only place she felt really at home was work. At least this break had taught her one thing, and that was how important her career was to her. Will might think her superficial, but at least she was prepared to go out and do a proper job, not sit around smiling all day like Dee.

'Are you sure you don't want to come?' Roger asked her the following Sunday. He and Beth were off to yet another barbecue, where they would meet all the people who had come to their barbecue the previous weekend, and Alice had opted out. 'Will might be there. They're bound to have invited everybody.'

If Will had wanted to see her, he knew where she lived. Alice had spent far too much of the week wondering if he would think about dropping round some time, and she was thoroughly disgusted with herself for being disappointed when he hadn't. She certainly wasn't about to go chasing after him at some party now!

'I don't think so, thanks,' she said, ultra-casual. She could hardly change her mind just because Roger had mentioned Will. What a giveaway *that* would be! 'I'll just stay here and finish my book.'

But, when Roger and Beth had gone, Alice sat with her book unopened on her lap and wished perversely that she had let herself be persuaded. After all, Will could hardly suspect her of chasing him if she just happened to bump into him at party, could he? She would have been able to see how he—how *Lily*, Alice corrected herself quickly—was getting on.

Then, of course, Dee might be at the party too. What could be more natural for Will to take her along since they were all living together? Did she *really* want to see that they were all getting along absolutely fine?

No, Alice acknowledged to herself, she couldn't honestly say that she did. Much better not to know. She was better off here.

Determinedly, she opened her book, but it was impossible to concentrate when all the time she was wondering if Roger and Beth had bumped into Will at the party, and, if they had, whether he would notice that she wasn't there. Would he ask where she was? Would he miss her?

'Oh, for heaven's sake!' Alice slammed her book shut, furious with herself. Will didn't even like her now. *Remember that little fact, Alice?* Why on earth would he miss her?

And why was she wasting her time even *thinking* about him?

When the doorbell went, she was so glad of the interruption that she leapt to her feet. It was Chantelle's day off, and she hurried to the door, not caring who it was as long as they distracted her from her muddled thoughts for a while.

Flinging open the door, she smiled a welcome, only to find the smile wiped from her face in shock as she saw who was standing there.

It was Will, with Lily a small silent figure beside him. The last people she had expected to see. The sight of them punched the breath from Alice's lungs, and, winded, she hung onto the door.

'Oh,' she said weakly. 'It's you.' She struggled to get some oxygen into her lungs but her voice still sounded thin and reedy. 'Hi…hello, Lily.'

''Lo,' Lily muttered in response.

Will cleared his throat. He looked as startled to see Alice as she was to see him, which was a bit odd given that he knew perfectly well that she was living there. 'Is Beth around?'

'No, she and Roger have gone to a party.' Alice had herself under better control now. It had just been the surprise. 'At the Normans, I think.'

'Damn, I'd forgotten about that …'

Will raked a hand through his hair and tried to concentrate on the matter in hand and not on how Alice had looked, opening the door, her face alight with a smile. Her hair swept back into its usual messy but stylish clip, and she was wearing loose trousers and a cool, sleeveless top. Her feet were thrust into spangled flip flops, and she looked much more relaxed than she had done at the party.

Much more herself.

'Is there a problem?' she asked.

He hesitated only for a moment. 'Yes,' he said baldly. Alice might be the last person he wanted to ask for help, especially under these circumstances, but he didn't have a lot of choice here. Too bad if she gave him a hard time about neglecting Lily. He had survived worse.

'There's been an accident on the project,' he said, his voice swift and decisive now that his mind was made up. 'I don't have many details yet, and I don't know how bad it is, but I need to go and see what's happened and if anyone's hurt. I can't take Lily with me until I know it's safe.'

'Where's Dee?' asked Alice, going straight to the heart of the problem as was her wont.

'She left yesterday.'

'Left?'

'She met some guy at the diving school last weekend.' Will wondered if he looked as frazzled as he felt. Probably, judging by Alice's expression. 'She's known him less than a week, but when he told her he was going back to Australia she decided to go with him.' He tried to keep his voice neutral, because he was afraid that if he let his anger and frustration show he wouldn't be able to control it.

Alice opened her mouth to ask how on earth that had happened, and then closed it again abruptly. Will was worried about Lily, worried about the accident. He didn't need her exclaiming and asking questions.

'Perhaps Lily could stay with me,' she said instead. 'You wouldn't mind keeping me company this afternoon, would you, Lily?'

Lily shook her head and, when Alice held out her hand, she took it after only a momentary hesitation.

'You go on,' Alice said to Will. 'I'll look after her until you get back.'

Astonished and relieved at her lack of fuss, Will could only thank her. He turned to go, but as he did he saw Alice nod imperceptibly down at his daughter. God, he'd almost forgotten to say goodbye! What kind of father did that make him?

'Goodbye, Lily,' he said awkwardly. If only he could be sure that if he crouched down and hugged her she would hug him back. 'Be good.' She was always good, though. That was the problem. 'I'll be back as soon as I can.'

Alice had to be one of the few people who knew less about parenting than he did, he thought bitterly as he reversed the car out of the drive and headed towards the project headquarters as fast as he could, but she was still able to make him realise how badly he was getting it wrong.

Alice, still able to wrong-foot him after all these years. Will shook his head. He had been waiting for her to take him to task for putting the project before his own child. He couldn't have blamed her if she'd pointed out that it was his fault for employing a silly girl like Dee who would run off and leave him in the lurch after barely more than a week as a nanny. She could have criticised him for not even thinking to say goodbye to Lily.

But she had done none of those things. She had recognized the problem and done exactly what he needed her to do. He would have to try and tell her later how much he appreciated it.

CHAPTER FIVE

'LILY'S asleep,' said Alice, opening the door to him nearly four hours later and motioning Will inside.

'Asleep?' He was instantly anxious. 'Is she OK?'

'Of course. She's just tired, and she dropped off a few minutes ago. It seems a shame to wake her just yet. Why don't you sit down and have a drink?' Her polite façade vanished as she watched Will drop into a chair. 'You look tired,' she added impulsively.

Will rubbed a hand over his face in a gesture so familiar that Alice felt a sharp pang of remembrance. 'I'm OK,' he said gruffly, but he was glad to sit down, he had to admit. The room was cool and quiet after the chaos at the hospital. 'Thanks,' he said as Alice came back with one of Roger's beers, and he drank thirstily.

'Was it a bad accident?' Alice asked. She sat on the end of the sofa, far enough away to be in no danger of touching him by accident, but not so far that it looked as if she was nervous about being alone with him.

'Bad enough.' Will lowered the bottle with a sigh. 'A couple of our younger members of staff had taken one of the project jeeps to the beach. It's their day off, and they had a few beers...you know what it's like. They're not supposed to take any of the vehicles unless they're on project business, but they're just lads.'

He grimaced, remembering the calls he had had to make to the boys' parents after he'd contacted the insurance company. 'Perhaps it's just as well they took one of our jeeps. It had our logo on the side, so when someone saw it had gone off the road they raised the alarm with the office, and the phone there gets switched through to me at weekends.'

'Are the boys OK?'

'They'll survive. They've both recovered consciousness, and the doctors say they're stable. The insurance company is making arrangements to fly them back to the UK, and the sooner that happens the better. The hospital here isn't equipped to deal with serious accidents.' He shook his head. Hospitals were grim enough places at the best of times.

'I'm glad I didn't have to take Lily there,' he said abruptly. 'I don't know how to thank you for looking after her, Alice.'

Alice avoided his eyes. 'It was no trouble,' she said with a careless shrug. 'Lily's good company.'

'Is she?' Will took another pull of his beer, unable to keep the bitterness from his voice. 'I can't get her to talk to me.'

'You need to give her time, Will. Everything's very new to her at the moment, and she's just lost her mother. You can't expect her to bounce back immediately.'

'I know, it's just…I don't know how to help her,' he admitted, the words wrenched out of him.

'You can help her best by being yourself. You're her father, and she knows that. Don't try too hard,' Alice told him. 'Let her get to know you.'

'Who made you such an expert on child care?' Will demanded roughly.

There was a tiny pause, and then, hearing the harshness of

his voice still echoing, he put down the beer and leant forward, resting his elbows on his knees and raking both hands through his hair. 'I'm sorry,' he said after a moment. 'That was uncalled for. Sorry.'

'You've got a lot on your mind at the moment,' said Alice after a moment.

'Still.' He straightened, and the grey eyes fixed on hers seemed to reach deep inside her and elicit a disturbing thrum. 'It's no excuse for rudeness.'

With an effort, Alice pulled her gaze away and reached for her lime juice with a hand that was not nearly as steady as she would have liked it to be.

'You're right, I don't know much about children,' she said. 'But Lily reminds me a lot of myself when I was younger. I was shy, the way she is, and I know what it's like—oh, not to lose my mother—but that feeling of not really knowing where you are or what you're doing there …' The golden eyes clouded briefly. 'Yes, I remember all that.'

'Is that why you were so angry with me at the party?'

Alice flushed. 'Partly. I shouldn't have said what I did, Will. I'm sorry, I was out of order. It wasn't any of my business.'

'No, you were right. I overreacted, mainly because you'd put your finger on all the things I felt most guilty and unsure about.' He smiled briefly. 'So it looks as if neither of us behaved quite as well as we might have done.'

He paused, his eyes on Alice, who had tucked her feet up beneath her and was curled into the corner of the sofa.

'What was the other reason?' he asked.

'Reason?' she said blankly.

'You said that was "partly" the reason you were angry,' he reminded her.

'Oh…' The colour deepened in Alice's cheeks, and she fiddled with the piping on the arm of the sofa. 'It's stupid, but

I suppose it was meeting you again after all this time. I was nervous,' she confessed.

'Me too,' said Will, and her eyes flew to his in disbelief.

'Really?'

He lifted his shoulders in acknowledgement. 'You were the last person I expected to see,' he told her with a rueful smile. 'I was completely thrown.'

'Oh,' said Alice with an embarrassed little laugh. 'Well… I'm glad it wasn't just me.'

'No.'

An awkward silence fell, and stretched at last into something that threatened to become even more difficult. Will drank his beer. Alice traced an invisible pattern on the arm of the sofa and kept her eyes lowered, but beneath her lashes her eyes kept sliding towards the fingers curled casually around that brown bottle.

Those fingers had once curved around her breast. They had drifted over her skin, stroking and smoothing and seeking. They had explored every inch of her, and late at night, when they had been intertwined with her own, she had felt safe in a way she never had before or since.

Alice's throat was dry, and that little thrum inside her was growing stronger and warmer, spreading treacherously along her veins and trembling at the base of her spine.

She reached forward for her glass with something like desperation. She shouldn't be remembering Will touching her, kissing her, loving her. They weren't the same people they had been then. Will was a father, and had more on his mind right now than remembering how the mere touch of his hands had been enough to melt her bones and reduce her to gasping, arching delight.

Sipping her lime juice, she sought frantically for something to say, but in the end it was Will who broke the silence.

'Roger and Beth still out?'

The question sounded too hearty to be natural, but Alice fell on it like a lifeline.

'Yes,' she said breathlessly. 'You know what party animals they are.'

'Why didn't you go?' Will asked her.

'I didn't feel like it.'

She didn't quite meet his eyes as she adjusted her hair clip. Telling him how she had dithered over the possibility of meeting him again wouldn't help. The atmosphere was taut enough as it was, even though they were both labouring to keep the conversation innocuous.

'I've spent all week going to coffee mornings and lunches, and we've been out to supper twice, and every time you meet the same people,' she said. 'To be honest, I had a much better time with Lily this afternoon.'

Will had finished his beer, and he looked around for a mat to put the bottle down on. 'What did you do with her?'

'Oh, you know…we just pottered around.'

'No, I really want to know,' he said. 'I'm going to have to spend more time with Lily, and it would help if I knew what she liked doing.'

'Well, she's very observant,' said Alice, glad to have moved the conversation into less fraught channels. 'And she's interested in things. We spent some time wandering around the garden, and she was full of questions, most of which I couldn't answer, like why the butterflies here are so colourful and why don't bananas grow in England… I think you'll make a scientist of her yet!'

Will's expression relaxed slightly. 'It's reassuring to know that she'll ask questions like that. She's always so quiet when she's with me.'

'She's not a chatterbox,' Alice agreed. 'But she'll talk if

she's got something to say. She got quite animated going through my wardrobe. She loves dressing up.'

'She gets that from her mother.' Will sounded faintly disapproving. 'Nikki was a great one for clothes. Her appearance was always very important to her.'

'Appearance is important to a lot of us,' said Alice, sensing the unspoken criticism in his comment. 'It doesn't always mean that you're superficial,' she added with a slight barb, remembering how his jibe at the party had stung.

'No, I suppose not,' said Will, although he didn't sound convinced, and Alice noticed darkly that he didn't take the opportunity of apologising for calling her superficial.

'It's perfectly normal for Lily to like dressing up,' she said with some tartness. 'Most little girls do. It doesn't mean she's condemned to life as an empty-headed bimbo! Some of us manage to dress well *and* hold down a demanding job.'

'You sound like Nikki,' he said, and from the bleak expression that washed across his face Alice gathered that it wasn't a compliment.

She longed to ask what Nikki had been like and what had gone wrong with their marriage, but it seemed inappropriate just then. Besides, she wasn't sure she wanted to know just how much she resembled Lily's mother.

'At least I stick at my jobs,' she pointed out with a slight edge. 'Unlike Dee.'

'Quite.' Will acknowledged the hit with a sigh. 'I should never have employed her, but she seemed so bright and lively that I thought she would be more fun for Lily to have around than some of the more experienced nannies. We obviously weren't fun enough for her, though,' he said, his mouth turning down at the memory of that dire week with Dee. 'She couldn't wait to go out as soon as I got home in the evening. I should have guessed she'd take the first chance to leave. I just didn't realise it would come quite so soon.'

'You couldn't have anticipated she'd throw up a good job to follow a guy she'd only known for a week,' said Alice, even as she wondered why she was trying to make him feel better.

Perhaps that was what superficial people did.

'If I'd been more experienced, I might have read the signs,' said Will. 'She was the only nanny the agency had on their books who could leave at such short notice, and now I know why!'

'What are you going to do now?'

Will put his arms above his head and tried to stretch out the tension in his shoulders. 'Get another nanny, I guess.' He leant back in his chair with a tired sigh. 'I'll have to get onto the agency tomorrow. I just haven't had a chance today.'

'It might take them some time to find someone suitable,' Alice pointed out. 'What happens in the meantime?'

'I'll just have to manage,' said Will, rubbing his face again. 'Lily's due to start school in a few weeks' time. I might be able to find someone locally who could help out until then, or maybe she could come to the project headquarters some days. It's not a very suitable place for a child, but I can hardly leave her on her own.'

'I'll look after her.'

The words were out of Alice's mouth before she had thought about them, and she was almost as startled by them as Will was. He sat bolt upright and stared at her.

'You?'

'Why not?' Some other person seemed to be controlling her speech. Was she really doing this? Arguing to look after Will's daughter for him? She must be mad! 'I managed this afternoon.'

'But …' Will looked totally thrown by her offer. Almost as thrown as Alice felt herself. 'You're on holiday,' he pointed out.

'I'm not suggesting I take on the job permanently. I'm just offering to help out until you can find a qualified nanny.'

'It's extraordinarily kind of you, Alice,' said Will slowly. 'But I couldn't possibly ask you to give up your holiday to look after Lily. You told me yourself that you were here for a complete break.'

'A break from routine is all I need.' Alice got to her feet and walked over to the sliding doors, trying to work out why it felt so important to persuade him.

'I thought I wanted to spend six weeks doing absolutely nothing,' she told him. 'When Beth told me about her life here, about the mornings by the pool, about the parties and the warmth and the sunshine, I was envious, jealous even.'

She remembered sitting at her desk, staring out at the rain and remembering Beth's bubbling enthusiasm. Tony hadn't been long gone, then, and she had still been at the stage of dreading going home to an empty flat.

'It was a bad time for me,' she told Will. She wasn't ready to tell him about Tony yet. 'The idea of just turning my face up to the sun and not thinking about anything for a while seemed wonderful, and when I got the chance to come I took it…'

'But?' Will prompted when she paused.

Alice turned back from the window to face him. 'But I'm bored,' she said honestly. 'It's different for Beth. She makes friends wherever she goes. She likes everybody, even if they're really dull, and she always sees the good side of people, but I'm …'

'… not like that?' he suggested, a hint of amusement in his eyes, and he looked suddenly so much like the Will she remembered that Alice's heart bumped into her ribs and she forgot to breathe for a moment.

'No,' she agreed, hugging her arms together and drawing

a distinctly unsteady breath. 'You know what I'm like. I'm intolerant, and I get impatient and restless if I'm bored.'

'They don't sound like ideal characteristics for a nanny,' Will pointed out in a dry voice, and she made herself meet his eyes squarely and not notice that disconcertingly familiar glint.

'Lily doesn't bore me,' she said. 'I like her. She reminds me of me, and I'm never bored when I'm on my own. Besides, I'm not planning on being a nanny. If this week has taught me anything, it's how important my career is. I need to work, and if I can't work, I need to do *something*.

'I enjoyed spending this afternoon with Lily,' she told Will. 'I'd much rather spend the next few weeks with her than twitter away at endless coffee mornings.'

'If that's how you feel, why don't you just cut short your trip?'

'Because I can't change my ticket. It was one of those special deals which means you can't get any refund if you change your flight. And Roger and Beth would be hurt if I said I was bored and wanted to go home. They've gone to so much trouble to make me welcome,' Alice added guiltily.

'They might be hurt if you choose to spend the rest of your time with Lily,' Will commented.

'I don't think so. Not if we present it as me helping you out.' Alice hoped she wasn't sounding *too* desperate, but, the more she thought about it, the more she liked the idea.

'I love Roger and Beth,' she said carefully. 'Of course I do. No one could be kinder or more hospitable, but I'm used to being independent and having my own space, making my own decisions.

'When you're a guest, you just fit in with everyone else,' she tried to explain. 'And I'm finding that harder than I thought. It's as if I'm completely passive. I don't decide what we're going to do, or what we're going to eat, or where we're going to go. I just tag along. At least if I was looking after Lily I'd have some say in how we spent the day.'

'I certainly wouldn't try and dictate what you did,' said Will. 'You know what would keep Lily happy better than I do. I do have a cook but I expect she'd be happy to make whatever you felt like.'

By the window, Alice brightened. 'You mean you're going to accept my offer?'

Will studied her eager face, puzzled by her enthusiasm and disconcerted by the way her mask of careful composure kept slipping to reveal the old, vivid Alice beneath.

'I don't know ...' he said slowly. 'It doesn't seem right somehow.'

'Is it because it's me?' she demanded. 'You wouldn't be hesitating if the agency had sent me out on a temporary assignment, would you?'

'Of course not. That would be a professional arrangement and I'd be paying you for your time.'

Alice shrugged. 'You can pay me if it makes you feel better, but it's not necessary. It's not as if I'm doing it for you, you know. I'd be doing it for me—and for Lily,' she added after a moment's thought.

Still, Will hesitated. Getting to his feet, he took a turn around the room, hands thrust into his pockets and shoulders hunched in thought. Finally he stopped in front of Alice.

'You don't think it would be a bit...difficult?' he asked. 'Living together again after all these years?'

'I'm not suggesting we sleep together,' said Alice, a distinct edge to her voice. 'Presumably Dee had her own room?'

'Of course.'

'Well, then.' She glanced at him and then away. 'It's different now, Will. What we had before is in the past. We agreed at the time that we would go our separate ways, and we have. There's no going back now.'

She was presenting it as something they had both decided together, but it hadn't been quite like that, not the way Will remembered it, anyway. It had been Alice who had wanted to end their relationship. 'Our lives are going in different directions,' she had said. 'Let's call it a day while we're still friends.'

'I think we both know that there's no point in trying to recreate what we had,' she was saying. 'I don't want that and neither do you, do you?'

'No,' said Will, after a moment. Well, what was he supposed to say—yes, I do? I do want that? I've never stopped wanting that?

That would have been a very foolish thing to say. He had tried to say it at Roger's wedding, and he wasn't putting himself through that again. He had enough problems at the moment without getting involved with Alice again. She was right; it was over.

'So what's the problem?' she asked him. 'It makes much more sense for you to have me living with you than some other woman who might fall in love with you and make things *really* awkward.'

It was her turn to pause while she tried to find the right words. 'We've both changed,' she said eventually. 'We're different people and we don't feel the same way about each other as we did then. We're never going to be lovers any more, but there's no reason why we couldn't learn to be friends, is there?'

Except that it was hard to be friends with someone whose taste you could remember exactly, thought Will. Someone whose body you had once known as well as your own, someone who'd been the very beat of your heart for so long.

With someone who'd made you happier than you had ever

been before. Someone who'd left your life empty and desolate when she had gone.

'It would only be for a few weeks,' Alice went on. 'And then I'd be gone. That wouldn't be too difficult, would it?'

'No,' said Will. 'We could do that for Lily.'

He had a feeling that it was going to be a lot harder than Alice made out, but it would be worth it for Lily. She liked Alice, that was clear, and Alice's presence would help her to settle down much more effectively than introducing yet another stranger into her life. He would just have to find his own way of dealing with living with Alice again.

And living without her once more when she had gone.

'All right,' he said, abruptly making up his mind. 'If you're sure, I expect Lily would love you to look after her until I can find a new nanny.'

He was glad that he had agreed when he saw Lily's face as the news was broken to her that Alice was going to stay with them for a while. She was never a demonstrative child, but there was no mistaking the way her dark eyes lit up with surprise and delight.

'You're going to live with us?'

'Just for a little while,' cautioned Alice. 'Until your dad can find you a new nanny.'

'Why can't you stay always?'

Will waited to see how Alice would handle that. It was a question he had wanted to ask her himself in the past. He had never understood why she had been so determined to end their relationship when they had been so good together. It was as if she had been convinced that everything would go wrong, but she hadn't been prepared to give it a chance to go right.

'Because I have to go home, Lily,' Alice told her. 'My life

is in London, not here. But until I do go back we'll have a lovely time together, shall we?'

Lily seemed to accept that. 'OK,' she said.

Alice was more nervous than she wanted to admit about how Beth would react to the news that she was moving out that night to live with Will and Lily. The last thing she wanted to do was to hurt Beth's feelings. But, once the situation about the missing nanny had been explained, Beth was very understanding, and even surprisingly enthusiastic about the idea.

'It sounds like the perfect solution,' she said, smiling, her gaze flickering with interest between Will and Alice. 'I'm sure you're doing the right thing.'

'I'm doing it for *Lily*,' said Alice pointedly. She didn't want Beth getting the wrong idea.

Beth opened her eyes wide. 'Of course,' she said. 'Why else?'

Roger was less convinced that it was a good idea. 'Are you sure about this, Alice?' he asked under his breath as they came to say goodbye.

'I'm sure,' she said. 'Don't worry about me.'

Roger glanced at Will. 'Maybe it's not you I'm worrying about.'

'We've talked about it,' said Alice firmly. 'It's going to be fine.'

'Well, you're a big girl now, so I guess you know what you're doing.' Roger swept her up into a hug. 'Look after yourself, though.'

'I'm only going up the road!'

'I'll still miss you. I've got used to coming home to find you drinking my gin.'

'I'll miss you, too. I always do.' Alice hugged her dearest friend, holding tightly onto his big bear strength, and her eyes were watery when he finally let her go.

'Oh, good God, she's going to cry!' exclaimed Roger in mock horror. 'Take her away, man!'

Will, who had observed that tight hug, thought it would not be a bad idea to get Alice away from Roger for a while. He was worried about Beth. At first glance, she seemed as bright and cheerful as ever, but on closer inspection Will thought there was a rather drawn look about her. It might be best all round if Alice came with him.

'Come on, then,' he said to Alice and Lily. 'Let's go home.'

They had decided that Alice might as well start her new role straight away, so she had already packed a bag by the time Beth and Roger got home. Now Will slung it in the back of his four-wheel drive and hoped to God he was doing the right thing.

Will's house had no pool, no air-conditioning, and was some way away from the exclusive part of St Bonaventure up on the hill where Roger and Beth lived in manicured splendour, but Alice felt instantly much more at home there. An unassuming wooden house set up on stilts, it had a wide verandah shaded by a corrugated-iron roof, and ceiling fans that slapped at the air in a desultory fashion.

It was set on a dusty, pot-holed road and an area of coarse tropical grass at the rear led down to a line of leaning coconut palms. 'The sea's just there,' said Will, pointing into the darkness. 'Go through the coconuts, cross a track and you're on the beach.'

He carried Alice's cases inside and put them in what had been Dee's bedroom. 'I need to make some calls, I'm afraid,' he said. 'I want to ring the hospital and see how the boys are, and then I'll have to talk to our head office in London. Lily, perhaps you could show Alice the house?' he suggested.

'That was a good idea, getting Lily to show me round,' Alice said to him later when they had eaten the light supper left by his cook and Lily had gone to bed. They were sitting out on the back verandah, listening to the raucous whirr of the insects in the dark and, in the distance, the faint, ceaseless suck of the sea upon the sand. Alice could just make out the gleam of water through the trunks of the palms. 'Knowing more about the house and where everything was made her realise that she was more at home than she thought. It was good for her to be able to explain everything to me,' Alice told Will. 'She might not have been talking much, but she's certainly been taking it all in.'

'I'm glad about that.' Will handed her a mug of coffee that he had made, unthinkingly adding exactly the right amount of milk. He hadn't forgotten how she took hers any more than she had forgotten how he liked his tea, Alice thought with an odd pang. She took the mug gingerly, taking care that her fingers didn't brush against his.

'This is going to be her home for a couple of years at least,' he went on, picking up his own mug and sipping at it reflectively. 'So she needs to feel that it's where she belongs.'

He paused to look sideways at Alice, who was curled up in a wicker chair, cradling her coffee between her hands. The light on the verandah was deliberately dim so as not to attract too many insects, but he could make out the high cheekbones that gave her face that faintly exotic look and the achingly familiar curve of her mouth. It was too hard to read her expression, though, and he wondered what she was thinking.

'I want to thank you, Alice,' he said abruptly. 'I know I didn't seem keen when you first suggested it, but I think it will be a very good thing for Lily to have you here.'

'I hope so,' she said.

'What about you? Do you think you'll be comfortable at least?' He glanced around him as if registering his conditions for the first time. 'I know it's not as luxurious as Roger's house.'

'No, but I like it better,' she said. Tipping back her head, she breathed in the heady fragrance of the frangipani that blossomed by the verandah steps. The wooden boards were littered with its creamy yellow flowers. 'This reminds me of the kind of places I lived in as a child.'

Will grimaced into his coffee. 'I'm not sure that's a good thing. You hated your childhood.'

'I hated the way my parents kept moving,' she corrected him. 'It wasn't the places or the houses—although we never lived anywhere as nice as this. It was the fact that I never had a chance to feel at home anywhere. My parents never stuck at anything. They had wild enthusiasms, but then they'd get bored, or things would go wrong, and they'd be off with another idea.'

She sighed. She loved her parents, but sometimes they exasperated her.

'I was shy to begin with. It was hard enough for me to make friends without knowing that in a year or so I'd be dragged somewhere new, where I'd have to learn a new language and make completely new friends. After a while, it didn't seem worth the effort of making them in the first place. It was easier if I was just on my own.'

It was her unconventional upbringing that had made Alice stand out from the other students. Will had noticed her straight away. It wasn't that she'd been eccentric or trying to be different. She'd dressed the same as everyone else, and she'd done what everyone else did, but there had been just something about the way she'd carried herself that drew the eye, something about those extraordinary golden eyes that had seen places that most of the other students barely knew existed.

Alice might complain about being endlessly uprooted by her parents, but continually having to adapt to new conditions had given her a self-sufficiency that could at times be quite intimidating.

It was a kind of glamour, Will had always thought, although Alice had hooted with laughter when he'd suggested it. 'There's nothing glamorous about living in a hut in the middle of the Amazon, I can tell you!' she had said.

'That's why I identify with Lily, I think,' she said now, sipping reflectively at her coffee. 'She's a solitary child too.'

'I know,' said Will, anxious as always when he thought about his daughter. 'But I hope she'll have a chance to settle down now. I should be here for two or three years.'

'And then?'

'Who knows?' he asked, a faint undercurrent of irritation in his voice. He wasn't her parents, moving his child around the world on a whim. 'It depends on my job. I'm not like you. I don't plan my life down to the last minute.'

'I've learnt not to do that either, now,' said Alice, thinking about Tony and the plans they had made together. 'There are some things you just can't plan for.'

Will arched a sceptical brow. 'I can't imagine you not planning,' he said. 'You were always so certain about what you wanted.'

'Oh, I still know what I want,' she said, an undercurrent of bitterness in her voice. 'The only thing that's changed is that now I'm not sure that I'll get it.'

CHAPTER SIX

'I GUESS that's something we all learn as we get older,' said Will. 'You can't always have what you want.'

His voice was quite neutral, but Alice found her head turning to look at him, and as their eyes met in the dim light she was suddenly very sure that he was thinking about Roger's wedding when he had told her what he wanted and she had said no.

She kept her own voice as light as possible. 'That's true, but perhaps we get what we need instead.'

'Do you think you've got what *you* need?'

Alice looked out into the darkness to where the Indian Ocean boomed beyond the reef.

'I've got a career,' she said, ignoring the little voice that said it wasn't much of one at the moment. 'I've got a flat and the means to pay my mortgage and earn my own living. I've got security. Yes, I'd say I've got everything I need.'

'Everything?' She didn't need to be looking at Will to know that his brows had lifted sardonically.

'What else would I need?'

'Let's say love, just for the sake of argument,' he said dryly. 'Someone you love and who loves you. Someone to hold you and help you and make you laugh when you're down.

Someone who can light up your world, and close it out when you're too tired to cope.'

Someone like he had been, Alice thought involuntarily, and swallowed the sudden lump in her throat.

'Why, Will, you've turned into a poet!' she said, deliberately flippant. 'Have they started doing an agony column in *Nature* and *Science Now*?'

'I read books too,' he said, unmoved by her facetiousness. 'So, do you?'

'Need love?' Alice leant down to put her coffee mug on the table between them. 'No, I don't. I used to think I did, but I've discovered I can manage quite well without it.'

'That's sad,' said Will quietly.

'Love would be great if you could rely on it, but you can't,' she said, wrapping her arms around herself as if she were cold. 'You can't control it. You think it's going to be wonderful and you trust it, and then you end up hurt and humiliated.' Her jaw set, remembering. 'If you want to be safe, you need to look after yourself, not put your whole happiness in someone else's hands.'

She glanced at Will. 'You asked me what I need. Well, I need to feel safe, and that's why I'm not looking for love any more.'

'You've been hurt,' he said, and she gave a short, bitter laugh.

'You can tell you've got a Ph.D., the speed you worked that one out!'

Will ignored her sarcasm. 'What happened?'

He thought at first that she wasn't going to answer, but suddenly Alice needed to tell him. It was too late to pretend that her life was perfect now. Will's clearly wasn't, so he might as well know the truth.

'I met Tony four years ago,' she began slowly. 'I'd had a few boyfriends, but there hadn't been anyone serious.'

There hadn't been anyone like Will. Alice pushed that thought aside and carried on. 'I hadn't exactly given up on meeting someone special, but I'd decided it probably wasn't going to happen. And then Tony came to work in my office.'

She paused, remembering that day. 'He was everything I'd ever wanted,' she said, oblivious to the wry look that passed over Will's face. 'We clicked immediately. We had so much in common. We liked doing the same things, and we wanted the same things out of life. I really thought he was The One,' she said, with an effort at self-mockery.

'Tony's careful,' she went on, even though she knew Will wouldn't understand. 'I felt safe with him. He's committed to his career, and he makes sure he invests his money sensibly. He thinks before he acts. He doesn't take stupid risks. That's why…'

She stopped, hearing her voice beginning to crack like a baby. Swallowing hard, she forced herself to continue. 'That's why I found it hard to believe that he would do something so out of character.'

'What did he do?' asked Will, part of him still grappling with disbelief at the idea that his lovely, vibrant Alice had decided after all to settle for safe, sensible and boring. He wouldn't have minded so much if she had fallen in love with someone wild, passionate and unsuitable, but how could she choose a man whose main attribute seemed to be a sensible approach to financial investments?

Alice drew a breath. 'He went out one day and fell in love at first sight.'

For a moment, Will was nonplussed. 'It happens,' he said, remembering that dizzy, dropping feeling he'd had the first time he'd laid eyes on Alice.

'Not to someone like Tony,' she said almost fiercely. 'We were together three and a half years, and I thought I knew him through and through. He was never impetuous. He never did anything without thinking it through.'

God, Tony sounded dull, thought Will. He wasn't a particularly reckless man himself, but he got the feeling that he would seem a positive daredevil next to Tony. What on earth had been his appeal for Alice?

'I couldn't believe it when he told me,' she was saying. 'He was very honest with me. He said that he'd thought that he did love me, but he realised when he met Sandi that he hadn't known what love was. It had taken us three years to decide that we would get married,' she added bitterly. 'It took him three minutes to know that he wanted to marry Sandi.'

'I'm sorry,' said Will, not knowing what else to say.

'Sandi's sweet and good and kind and pretty,' Alice went on. 'She really is,' she insisted, seeing Will's sceptical look. 'It's really hard to dislike her, and, believe me, I've tried. No one who meets her is at all surprised that Tony fell for her. The only surprising thing is that he thought he loved *me* for so long. Sandi's about as different from me as she could be.'

'She doesn't sound very interesting,' Will said, but Alice wasn't to be consoled.

'Tony doesn't want interesting. Interesting is too much like hard work,' she said. 'I thought I was making an effort for him, but it turned out I was "challenging" him,' she remembered, bitterness creeping back into her voice. 'I don't know how. I didn't think I had particularly high expectations, but there you go. Apparently I'm very demanding.'

'You're not easy,' Will agreed. 'But you're worth the effort. If Tony couldn't be bothered to make that effort, you're better off without him.'

'It didn't feel that way,' said Alice bleakly. 'We have lots of friends in common, so I see Tony with Sandi quite often. I don't think he's regretted his decision for a minute. In fact, I think he wakes up in a cold sweat sometimes, realising what a narrow escape he had!'

She tried to sound as if she didn't mind, but Will could hear the thread of hurt in her voice.

'They're still together, then?'

'They got married last week,' said Alice, her eyes on the dull gleam of the sea through the darkness. 'The day I met you at Roger and Beth's party.'

Will remembered how tense she had been that day. Alice had always been too proud to show how much she hurt inside. He should have guessed that something more than the passage of time was wrong, but he had been too shaken by his own reaction to give any thought to hers.

'I'm sorry,' he said again. 'It must have been difficult for you.'

Alice lifted her chin. She had always hated any suspicion of pity. 'I survived,' she said curtly. 'But that's why I'm doing without love at the moment.'

'You know, we all get hurt sometimes,' said Will mildly. 'Some of us more than once.'

'Once is enough for me,' said Alice.

Silence fell. They sat together in the hot, still night, each wrapped in their own thoughts, while the insects shrilled frantically in the darkness and the lagoon whispered onto the sand.

Alice was very aware of Will beside her. It was strange, being with him again, feeling that she knew him intimately, and yet hardly at all. He wasn't the same man he had been, she reminded herself for the umpteenth time. He was harder, more contained than he had been, and he had grown out of his lankiness to a lean, solid strength.

Her eyes slid sideways under her lashes to rest on the austere profile. She couldn't see them in the darkness but she knew there were new lines creasing his eyes, a tougher set to his jaw, a sterner line to his mouth.

That capacity for stillness was the same, though. She had often watched him sitting like that, his body relaxed but alert, and envied his ability to withdraw from the chaos and just be calm. She had loved his competence, his intelligence, the ironic gleam in the humorous grey eyes. Even as a young man, he had had an assurance that was understated, like everything else about Will, but quite unmistakeable.

There was something insensibly reassuring about his quiet presence. Whatever happened, you felt that Will could deal with it and everything would be all right. Even now, after everything that had happened, he made her feel safe.

If only that was all he had made her feel! The initial attraction she had felt for the ordinary-looking student had deepened into a dangerous passion that made Alice uneasy. She didn't like feeling out of control, and the strength of her emotions scared her.

Will had started out a good friend, a good companion, and he had become a good lover, but soon it went beyond even that. Alice was out of her depth. She didn't like the feeling of needing him, of not feeling quite complete without him. All her experience had taught her to rely on herself, and she had forced herself to resist the lure of binding herself to him for ever.

Because she had been so in love she hadn't seen that they wanted very different things out of life. The future Will enthused about hadn't been the one Alice had dreamed of. She had yearned all her life for security, and that had been the one thing Will couldn't offer. He'd wanted to continue his research, to work wherever he could find a coral reef, to do what he could to protect them. She'd wanted a wardrobe, somewhere she could hang up her clothes and never have to unpack them. She'd wanted a place she could call her own. She'd been sick of scrimping and saving to put herself through university. She'd been sick of window shopping. If she saw a pair of wonderful shoes in a window, she wanted to be able to go in and buy them.

There were no shoe shops on coral reefs. If she'd married Will, as he had asked her to, she'd have had to give up all her dreams to live his. Alice had decided that she couldn't, wouldn't, do that.

She had made the right decision, she told herself, but there was no denying that the physical attraction was still there. It was very hard to explain. There was nothing special about the way Will looked. He had a lean, intelligent face that could under no circumstances be called handsome, but the contrast between the severe mouth and the humorous grey eyes made him seem more attractive than he actually was.

The first time Alice had seen Will, she hadn't been conscious of any instant physical attraction. Later, that seemed strange. She'd thought he was nice, but it was only as she'd got to know him that she'd begun to notice those things that made him uniquely Will: the firmness of his chin, the texture of his skin, the angle of his jaw. The way the edges of his eyes creased when he smiled.

Once she had start noticing, of course, it had been impossible to stop. It hadn't been long before Alice had found her body utterly in thrall to his, and she'd only had to look at his mouth for her breath to shorten and for her entrails to be flooded with a warmth that spread through her until it lodged, tingling and quivering with excitement, just beneath her skin.

The way it was doing now.

Alice tucked her feet beneath her once more and drew herself in, willing the jangling awareness to fade. 'It's not enough,' she had told Will at Roger's wedding, and she knew that she had been right. If she let herself be sucked back into those dark, swirling depths of sexual attraction, she would lose control of her life and her self completely, and the last ten years would have been for nothing.

She swallowed, hard. 'So, what about you?' she asked to break the lengthening silence. 'Do you know what you want?'

For years Will would have been able to say instantly that he wanted her. And then he would have said that he wanted to forget her. Now …

'Not really,' he said slowly. 'I've learnt not to want anything too specific. I don't want a Porsche or a knighthood or to win a million pounds. But I want other things, I suppose,' he went on, thinking about it.

'I want to keep Lily safe. I want her to grow up with a sense of joy and wonder at the world around her. I don't want her to be afraid of it.' He turned his head to look at Alice. 'I don't want her to end up frightened of love or too proud to admit that she needs other people.'

'Oh, so you don't want her to end up like me?' Alice asked flippantly, but there was no answering smile on Will's face as he met her gaze steadily.

'No,' he agreed. 'I want her to be happy.'

Was that really how he saw her—unhappy and afraid? Alice lay in bed that night, scowling into the darkness, hating the memory of the pity she had seen in Will's face. She didn't need him to be sorry for her. She was fine. She could look after herself. She didn't need anybody.

She had thought that she needed Tony, and look where that had got her. She had placed him at the centre of her life and told herself that she was safe at last. Tony hadn't made her head whirl with excitement, it was true, but it wasn't passion that Alice was looking for. She had had that with Will, and the power of those unmanageable emotions had left her uneasy and out of control. With Tony, she had felt settled and as if her future was safe at last. It had been a wonderful feeling.

Until Sandi had come along, and her carefully constructed world had fallen apart.

All those years she had dreamed of feeling secure, and with one meeting it had been shattered. Was it the loss of that dream that hurt more than losing Tony himself? Alice wondered for the first time. And did that mean that she had never really loved Tony at all?

For some reason, it was that thought that made Alice cry in a way she hadn't been able to cry since Tony had left. Trapped in a straitjacket of hurt and humiliation, she had taken refuge in a stony pride, but all at once she could feel the careful barriers she had erected around herself crumbling, and she lay under the mosquito net and wept and wept until at last she fell asleep.

Her eyes were still puffy when she woke the next morning, but she felt curiously released at the same time. Having spent her childhood trying not to let her parents guess how unhappy she was, Alice felt uncomfortable with crying. Until now, it had just seemed another way of admitting that everything was out of control, and she'd been afraid that, once she started, she might never be able to stop.

But this morning it felt as if a heavy hand had been lifted from her heart.

Perhaps she should try tears more often, Alice thought wryly.

Will had gone by the time she got up. She found Lily in the kitchen with the cook, a severe-looking woman called Sara. Alice was quite intimidated by her, but Lily seemed to accept her and was already picking up some words of the local language, a form of French Creole.

Alice was relieved not to have to face Will just yet. She might feel better for a good cry, but she had told him more than she wanted about herself last night, and now she felt exposed. At least she hadn't cried in front of him—that was something—but he had still been sorry for her, and that wasn't a feeling Alice liked at all.

She spent the morning exploring the garden with Lily, and together they crossed the track to the beach. In the daylight, the lagoon was a translucent, minty green, its surface ruffled occasionally by a cat's paw of breeze from the deep blue ocean that swelled and broke against the protecting reef. The leaning coconut palms splashed the white sand with shade, but it was still very hot and Alice was glad to keep on the shoes she had put on to pick her way through the coarse husks and roots that littered the ground beneath the trees.

She had bought the sandals on impulse at a market the previous summer, and Lily was frankly envious. They were cheap but fun, their garish plastic flowers achingly bright in the dazzling sunshine.

'I wish I could have some shoes like that,' said Lily wistfully.

'Let's see if we can find you some in town,' Alice said without thinking, and Lily's face lit up.

'*Could* we?' She sounded dazzled by the prospect.

'We'll go this afternoon,' said Alice.

'Look what I've got,' Lily said to Will when he got home that evening, and she lifted one foot so that he could admire her new shoes.

There hadn't been a great deal of choice in town—St Bonaventure would have to give some thought to modernising its shops if it wanted to attract large numbers of tourists and relieve them of their money, Alice thought—but they had found a pair of transparent pink sandals in Lily's size, and she could hardly have been more delighted if they were Manolo Blahniks.

Will shot a glance at Alice before studying the shoe Lily was showing him so proudly. 'They're very…pink,' he said after a moment.

'I know,' said Lily, deeply pleased.

'Lily and I thought we'd do a spot of shopping,' said Alice, who could tell that Will was considerably less delighted with the shoes but was trying hard not to show it.

'So I see.'

Lily looked earnestly up at her father. 'Alice is good at shopping,' she said, and Will's jaw tightened.

'There are more important things to be good at in life than shopping,' he said.

'Did you have to be quite so crushing?' Alice demanded crossly much later, when Lily was in bed. 'She was so thrilled with her shoes. It wouldn't have killed you to have shown some interest.'

'How can you be *interested* in a pair of shoes?' snarled Will, who was in a thoroughly bad mood, exacerbated by guilt at so comprehensively pricking his daughter's balloon earlier.

It had been the first time Lily had volunteered any information when he'd come home. Part of him had been ridiculously moved that she had come to show him her new shoes without prompting. She had been chattier than usual, too, but he had had to go and spoil things by his thoughtless comment.

Will sighed. He was very tired. It had been a long day, dealing with the fall-out from yesterday's accident, and it hadn't helped that he had slept badly the night before. His mind had been churning with what Alice had told him about her broken engagement. In the small hours, Will had had to acknowledge that he didn't like the fact that Tony had obviously been so important to her.

It was Tony who had given her what she wanted, Tony she was missing now. Alice could say all she wanted about not needing anybody; it was clear that she had loved Tony, and that he was the one she was always going to regret. Will knew exactly what that felt like.

He was sorry, of course, that she had been hurt so badly. But his pity was mixed with resentment at the years *he* had spent believing that he would never find anyone who could make him feel the way she did, the years spent hoping that somehow, somewhere, she was missing him too, and was sorry that she had ended things when she had.

And all the time she had been in love with Tony, dull, safe, sensible Tony who had broken her heart! Will was furious with her for making it so clear how ridiculous his fantasy had been all along, and more furious with himself for caring.

As if that wasn't enough of a slap in the face, now she was the one who was getting through to Lily. It was Alice who was making the bond with his daughter that should really be his, and he resented that too. Will knew that he was being unreasonable and unfair, and he was ashamed of himself, but there it was, something else to add to the mix of his already confused feelings about her.

The next few weeks were going to be even harder than he had feared. Lily went to bed early, which meant that there would just be the two of them alone together every evening like this. Alice still stirred him like no other woman he had ever met. She made him feel angry, and resentful and regretful and grateful and irritated and amused and sympathetic and muddled and disappointed and exhilarated and aroused, often all at the same time. And all it took was for her to turn her head and he was pierced by such joy at her presence that it drove the breath from his lungs.

'Look,' he said, 'I'm sorry I wasn't more enthusiastic about the shoes. I know she likes them. I just don't think it's a good idea for you to encourage her to think that happiness lies in shopping.'

Alice was exasperated. 'I bought her a pair of cheap shoes,' she said tightly, and was aware, deeply buried, of relief that

Will was being so objectionable. It was much easier to be cross than to be aware of him and his mouth, his hands and the way he made her *feel* again. 'It wasn't a philosophical statement, and it won't turn her into a raging materialist. It was just a present, and not a particularly expensive one at that.'

'It's not about the money,' said Will irritably. 'It's about giving her false expectations of the kind of life she's going to have now. Nikki used to buy her things the whole time—toys, clothes, the latest brands, whatever made her feel better for being away at work so much—but that's not going to happen now. I'm not going to try and buy Lily's love, even if I had the time to do it. Little shopping trips like today's will just remind Lily of a life that's gone, and I'm afraid it will just make it harder for her to settle down here.'

'There's a difference between buying affection and giving your child some security,' snapped Alice. 'Lily's been wrenched out of the only life she's ever known. Where *are* all these toys and clothes that her mother bought for her? Did it not occur to you that she might like a few familiar things around her? Or would that have been making things too easy for her? I suppose you thought what she really needed was a clean break and the equivalent of an emotional boot camp to help her settle!'

'Of course not,' said Will stiffly. 'It's true I only brought what I could carry this time, but all her other things are being shipped out. They should arrive in a couple of weeks.'

'Oh,' said Alice, wrong-footed. She had been ready to whip herself into a fury at his stupidity and intransigence. 'Well… good,' she finished lamely.

'Is there anything else she needs—apart from pink shoes, that is—until the shipment arrives?'

'She could do with more to keep her occupied during the day.' Alice was glad that Will had given her the opening. She had intended to raise it, but was afraid she might have pushed him a bit too far to suggest it herself. 'If I didn't think you'd throw a fit at the idea of going to the shops again, I'd suggest getting her some books and maybe some paper and crayons.'

'If I give you some money, will you take her and let her choose whatever she wants?'

'What?' She clapped a hand to her chest and opened her eyes wide. 'You mean we're going to be allowed to go *shopping*?'

Will clamped down on his temper, not without some difficulty. 'For things Lily really needs,' he said repressively. 'I don't want it spent on rubbish.'

'Heavens, no! We don't want to risk Lily having something silly that would give her pleasure, do we?' Alice got up in a swish of skirt. 'That would be spoiling her, and we can't have *that*!'

He had handled that all wrong, thought Will glumly as she swept off saying that she was going to read in her room. He had to stop letting her get to him like this. He needed to forget that she was Alice and treat her the way he would any other nanny. Dee hadn't wound him up this way, and she hadn't done nearly as good a job as Alice. Somehow he would have to find a way to start again.

Alice was decidedly frosty the next morning, and Will's nerve failed at the thought of a tricky discussion before breakfast, but he was determined to make amends when he came home. He left work as early as he could, and found Alice and Lily on the back verandah playing cards.

Hesitating behind the screen door, he looked at the two heads bent close together over the little table, and his chest tightened so sharply that he had to take a deep breath before he pushed open the door.

At the sound of the door banging to behind him, Lily looked up with a shy smile. She didn't cry 'Daddy!' or throw herself into his arms, but it was such a big step for her that

Will felt enormously heartened. Alice was looking aloof, but that didn't bother him. He knew he would have to work harder to win her round, but in the meantime he was content to go over and ruffle Lily's dark hair.

'Hello,' he said with a smile. 'What are you playing?'

'Memory.'

'Who's winning?'

'Alice is,' Lily admitted reluctantly.

That was typical of Alice. She would never patronise a six-year-old by letting her win. When Lily *did* win, her victory would be the sweeter.

'It won't be easy to beat her,' Will warned Lily. 'She's got a good memory.'

Too good a memory, Alice thought, trying not to notice how the smile softened his face. She didn't want to be able to remember too well at the moment. It would be much easier if she could forget the times she and Will had played cards together. Neither of them had had any money as students, and they hadn't been able to go out very often, but Alice had been perfectly happy to stay at home with him, to sit on the floor and play cards, while outside the rain beat against the windows.

Once, when she'd got a distinction for an essay, Will had taken her out to dinner to celebrate. He had only been able to afford an old-fashioned brasserie on the outskirts of town with plastic tablecloths and a dubious taste in décor, but it had still been one of the best meals Alice had ever had. She wanted to forget that, the way she wanted to forget the long walks along winter beaches, the lazy Sunday mornings in bed, all those times when they had laughed until it hurt. She wanted to forget the feel of those hands curving over her body, to forget the taste of his mouth, of his skin. The last thing she wanted was to be able to remember the sweet, shivery, swirling and oh-so-seductive pleasure they had found in each other night after night.

She wanted to remember why it had been such a good idea to end it all.

Will was still talking to Lily. 'That was a good idea to buy cards.'

'We went shopping again.' Lily eyed her father with a certain wariness after his unenthusiastic response to her shoes the day before, but he kept his smile firmly in place.

'Did you buy anything else?'

'Some books.'

'Show me what you bought.'

Lily ran off quite willingly to find the books, and Will glanced at Alice, who immediately turned away, mortified to have been caught watching him.

'Don't lift your chin at me like that,' he said. 'I know I deserve it, but I really am sorry. I was in a bad mood yesterday, and I shouldn't have taken it out on you and Lily, but I did.'

Alice's chin lowered a fraction.

'I'm truly grateful to you, Alice, for what you've done. You've made a huge difference to Lily already, and I know I'm going to have to try harder to make things work if we're going to spend the next month together. Say you'll forgive me,' he coaxed. 'It'll make it much easier for us all if you do!'

The chin went down a bit further.

'Would you like me to go down on my knees and apologise?'

'That won't be necessary,' said Alice with as much dignity as she could muster. She wished he would go back to being grumpy and disagreeable, but she could hardly sulk for a month. 'Apology accepted.'

'I really am sorry, Alice,' Will said quietly, and, in spite of herself, Alice's head turned until she met his steady gaze.

That was something else she remembered—how those grey eyes could tip her off balance so that she felt as if she was toppling forward and tumbling down into their depths falling out of time and into a place where there was nothing but Will and the slow, steady beat of her heart and the boom of her pulse in her ears.

And when she had managed to wrench her eyes away it had almost been a shock to find, like now, that the world had kept turning without her. Alice had once been sitting on a train, waiting for it to depart and watching the train beside them turn into a blur of carriages as they pulled out of the station. She had never forgotten the jarring shock of realising that it was another train that had left, and hers hadn't moved at all. As the last carriage had disappeared and she'd seen the platform once more, it had felt as if her train had jerked to a sudden, sickening halt. It was the same feeling she had now.

'Let's both try harder,' she muttered.

'All right,' said Will. 'Let's do that.'

CHAPTER SEVEN

'DO YOU want to see my books?'

It was a tiny comfort that Will seemed as startled as Alice was by Lily's reappearance. She was clutching a pile of books to her chest and watching them with a doubtful expression, as if sensing something strange in the atmosphere.

'Of course I do.' Will forced a smile. 'Let's have a look.'

Lily's face was very serious as she stood by his chair and handed him the books one by one. Will examined them all carefully. 'This looks like a good one,' he said, pulling out a book of fairy stories. He glanced at his daughter. 'Would you like me to read you a story?'

Lily hesitated and then nodded, and, feeling as if she were somehow intruding on a private moment, Alice got to her feet. She suspected that this was the closest Will had ever been to Lily, and the first time he read her a story should be something special for both of them.

'That sounds like a good idea,' she said, firmly quashing the childish part of her that felt just a tiny bit excluded. 'You two read a story together, and I'll go and heat up the supper Sara left for us. She left very strict instructions, and I'm frightened of what she'll say if I get it wrong!'

Alice lingered in the kitchen, giving them time alone

together. It wasn't a bad thing for her to have some time to herself too, she reflected. She had spent all day feeling furious with Will, and there had been something almost comforting in that, but all he had had to do was say sorry and look into her eyes and her anger had crumbled. Like a town without a wall, she was left without defences, and it made her feel oddly vulnerable and uneasy. Will shouldn't still be able to do that to her.

Oh, this was silly! Alice laid the table with unnecessary vehemence, banging down the knives and forks, cross with herself for making such a fuss about nothing. She should be glad that Will had apologised and was obviously prepared to be reasonable. She *was* glad for Lily's sake, if not her own. They couldn't have spent the next month arguing with each other. That would have been no example to set a six-year-old.

It would be so much easier if she could just think of Will as Lily's father, if she could wipe out the memories of another time and another place. It was all very well to tell him that she wanted to be friends, but that was harder than she'd thought it would be.

Alice sighed. Her feelings about Will weren't simple. They never had been and they never would be, and she might as well accept that. Nothing had changed, after all. She had meant what she had said. When her holiday was over, she was going home and she was starting life afresh on her own. No more looking back, no more wanting something from love that it just couldn't give.

When Alice went back out onto the verandah, Will and Lily were sitting close together on the wicker two-seater. Will's arm rested loosely around his daughter and she was leaning into him, listening intently to the story.

Reluctant to disturb them, Alice sat down quietly and listened too. The sun was setting over the ocean, blazing through the trunks of the palm trees, and suffusing the sky with an unearthly orange glow in the eerie hush of the brief tropical dusk. Lily's face was rapt. Will's deep voice resonated in the still air and, watching them, Alice felt a curious sense of peace settle over her. Time itself was suspended between day and night, and suddenly there was no future, no past, just now on the dusty wooden verandah.

'… and they lived happily ever after.' Will closed the book, and his smile as he looked down at his daughter was rather twisted. It was sad that Lily already knew that things didn't always end as happily as they did in stories.

'Did you like that?' he asked, and Lily nodded. 'We could read another one tomorrow, if you like,' he said casually, not wanting her to know how much it had meant to him to have her small, warm body leaning against him. It was like trying to coax a wild animal out of its hiding place, he thought. He wanted desperately for her to trust him, but he sensed that, if he was too demonstrative, she would retreat once more.

'OK,' she said. It wasn't much, but Will felt as if he had conquered Everest.

It was all getting too emotional. Alice had an absurd lump in her throat. Definitely time to bring things down to earth. 'Let's have supper,' she said.

'You're starting to make a real bond with her,' she said to Will.

Lily was in bed, the supper had been cleared away, and by tacit agreement she and Will had found themselves back on the verandah. She had thought about excusing herself and spending the evening reading in her room, but it was too hot, and anyway that would look as if she was trying to avoid him, which would be nonsense. They had cleared the air, and there was no reason for them to be awkward together.

Besides, she liked it out here. It reminded her of being a child, when she would lie in bed and listen to the whirr and click and scrape of the insect orchestra overlaid by the comforting sound of her parents' voices as they sat and talked in the dark outside her room.

She had been thinking of her father a lot this evening. He used to read to her the way Will had read to Lily earlier. He would put on extraordinary voices and embellish the stories wildly as he went along, changing the ending every time, so that Alice had never been quite sure how it was going to turn out. No wonder she had grown up craving security, Alice thought with a rueful smile. She hadn't even been able to count on books to stay the same until she could read them for herself!

Funny how she kept thinking of her childhood here. Normally, she kept those memories firmly buried, but she was conscious that she was remembering it not with her usual bitterness and frustration, and not with nostalgia either, but, yes, with a certain affection. Perhaps she should have remembered more of the good times as well as the bad.

'Lily's learning to trust you,' she went on, and Will leant back in his chair and stretched with a sigh that was part relief, part weariness.

'I hope so,' he said. 'Just doing something simple like reading a story makes me realise how much time I've missed with her. I've got a lot of catching up to do.'

Alice hesitated. 'How come you're such a stranger to her?' she asked curiously, hoping that she wasn't opening too raw a wound. 'Didn't you want a child?'

Will glanced at her and then away. 'Do you want the truth?' he said. 'When Nikki first told me that she was pregnant, I was appalled. Lily was the result of a doomed attempt to save a failing marriage. That's not a good reason to bring a child into the world. Nikki had already made arrangements to leave when she found out she was pregnant. So, no, I didn't want a child then.'

'But Nikki decided to keep the baby?'

'Yes. I don't know why, to be honest,' said Will. 'She couldn't wait to get back to her career, and as far as I could make out Lily spent more time with her grandparents than she did with her mother. Nikki made it very clear that it was her decision whether or not to keep the baby, and I had to respect that. I accepted my responsibility to support the child, but I couldn't really imagine what it would be like to be a father,' he admitted. 'I hadn't been involved in the pregnancy the way most fathers are. I didn't get to see the first scan, or go to antenatal classes. I was just someone who would be handing over a certain sum of money every month.'

'Would you rather Nikki had chosen not to have the baby?' Alice asked curiously.

'There was a time when I thought that would have been the best solution,' said Will. 'But then a funny thing happened. Nikki didn't want me there at the birth, but she did let me see Lily a couple of days later.'

'You cared enough to see her, anyway.'

He looked out at the night. 'I can't honestly say I cared, not then,' he said slowly. 'I felt responsible, that's all. Nikki was in London by then, and I was working in the Red Sea, but my child was being born. I couldn't just pretend it wasn't happening, could I?'

Some men might have done, reflected Alice, but not Will.

'So I went to visit,' he went on, unaware of her mental interruption. 'I guess Nikki thought that if she wanted me to pay maintenance she would have to let me see my own child, but she wasn't exactly welcoming. Fortunately, there was a nice nurse there. I'm not sure whether she knew the situation, or just thought I was a typically nervous first-time father, but before I could say anything she picked Lily up and put her in my arms and—'

He stopped, and in the dim light Alice could just see that his mouth was pressed into a straight line that was somehow more expressive of the feelings he was suppressing than a dramatic show of tears and emotion would have been.

'…And I felt…' he began again when he had himself under control, only to falter to a halt again. 'I can't really describe how I felt,' he admitted after a moment. 'I looked down at this tiny, perfect little thing and just stared and stared. She was so new and so strange, and yet I knew instantly—deep in my gut—that she was part of me.

'I've never felt anything like it before,' he said. 'It was such a strong feeling, it was like a tight band around my chest, and I could hardly breathe with it. It was too painful to be happiness, and there was terror in there too, but it was a wonderful feeling too… I don't know what it was.'

Surprised at how moved she was, Alice managed a smile. 'It sounds like love,' she said, lightly enough, and Will turned his head to look at her for a long, intense moment.

'Yes,' he said after a moment. 'I suppose that's what it was. But not love the way—'

He had so nearly said *the way I loved you.* Will caught himself up just in time.

'It's not the same as the love between a man and a woman,' he finished smoothly.

'Of course not,' said Alice. 'But it's still love. I've never had a child, but I recognized the feeling you described straight away.'

She remembered lying in bed next to Will and feeling just that mixture of terror and wonder, a feeling so intense that it was almost pain. Its power had seemed dangerous, overwhelming, uncontrollable, and in the end she had run away from it. She had been a coward, Alice knew, but at the time it had seemed the sensible thing to do.

And now… Well, there was no point in looking back. No

point in wondering what it would have been like if she had given in to that feeling instead of fighting it, if she had chosen love rather than security. She and Will might have had a child together. She would have discovered for herself how it felt to hold a child in her arms.

She wouldn't have been able to run away from *that* feeling.

Aware that she was drifting perilously close to regret, Alice gave herself a mental shake. She had made her own choices, and she would have to live with the consequences.

'I don't think Lily knows that you love her that much,' she said, breaking the silence.

'How could she?' said Will. 'I've hardly seen her since she was a baby. Nikki had already started the divorce process before Lily was born.'

'You'd think the baby would have brought you together,' Alice commented.

'I would have been prepared to give it another go for Lily's sake, but I suspect Nikki was right when she said that we both knew it wasn't going to work, so we'd better accept reality sooner rather than later.'

Will shifted shoulders restlessly, as if trying to dislodge the memory pressing onto them. Of course, that was what Alice had said too. *It'll never work. Let's call it a day while we're still friends. It's not worth even trying.* At least Nikki had taken the risk of marrying him. Alice hadn't even had the guts to give it a go.

'So you didn't contest the divorce?'

'No.' He shook his head. 'Our marriage was a mistake. Nikki was right about that. We should never have got married in the first place.'

'Why did you, then?' asked Alice, who had no patience with people who didn't think through the consequences of their actions. Of course, sometimes you could think about things too much, and you ended up missing opportunities, but Will was an intelligent man, and marriage was a serious business. It wasn't the kind of thing you fell into *by mistake*.

The sharpness in her voice made Will glance at her, but he didn't answer immediately. How could he tell Alice how hard he had tried to find someone else after she had given him that final 'no' at Roger's wedding? How every woman he'd met had seemed either twee or colourless in comparison to her? Nikki had been the first woman he'd met with a strength of personality to match hers. Seduced by the notion of wiping Alice from his memory once and for all, Will had convinced himself that he was falling in love with Nikki's forcefulness and vivacity, and he had been too eager to find out what she was really like until it was too late.

'I think I fell in love with the idea of Nikki, rather than with the person she really was,' he said at last. 'And I think she did the same.'

Alice opened her mouth to tell him it had been madness to even think about marrying an idea, but then closed it abruptly. Hadn't she done the same with Tony, after all? Tony had represented something that she had always yearned for, but she hadn't really known him. If she had, she might not have been so unprepared when he'd met Sandi.

'It was a holiday romance that got out of hand,' Will went on. 'She came out to the Red Sea to learn how to dive, and when we met she was incredibly enthusiastic about diving and the reef. I saw that she was fun, pretty, vivacious…and I think she saw me as someone very different from her friends and business associates in London.'

Alice could imagine it all very clearly. To Nikki, bored with men in suits and ties, escaping from a cold, grey London, Will must have seemed hard to resist with his wind-tanned skin and the glitter of sunlit sea in his eyes. He would have been a step up, too, from the surfers and beach bums. Will's shorts and T-shirts might have been as faded from the sun as theirs, but he had an air of competence and assurance that gave him the kind of authority other men had to put on suits to acquire.

'So you were both carried away by the sea and the stars?' she suggested, with just a squeeze of acid in her voice.

'You could say that,' Will agreed dryly. 'And of course, once reality set in, the sea and the stars weren't enough. Nikki was full of how she wanted to start a new life with me, but it didn't take long before she was bored, and then she started to resent me for "making" her give up her career in London.'

His mouth twisted. 'It wasn't a good time. We tried to patch things up—hence Lily—but in the end it was obvious it wasn't going to work. Nikki wanted to pick up her career where she'd left off, and the truth was that by then I wanted out of the marriage too. I just didn't count on how Lily's birth would change things.'

'It must have made everything more complicated,' said Alice, and he gave a mirthless laugh.

'You could say that. Nikki insisted on having full custody of Lily, and I was prepared to accept that. What I wasn't prepared to accept was not having any access to my daughter at all.'

'No access? But that's completely unreasonable!' Alice protested, shocked. '*And* unfair!'

Will shrugged. 'Unreasonable…unfair… You can shout all you like, but, when you're up against the kind of hot-shot lawyers Nikki hired, saying that it's unfair doesn't get you very far. For two years she refused to communicate with me except through the intimidating letters her lawyers would send me.'

'But why would she be like that? You'd have thought she'd have wanted her child to grow up knowing its father!'

'I don't know.' Will rubbed a weary hand over his face. 'The only thing I can think was that she was afraid I'd somehow take Lily away, but I wouldn't have done that, and she had no grounds for suspecting that I would.'

'I'm sorry,' said Alice, appalled at what Will had been through. 'It must have been very hard for you.'

'I didn't react quickly enough.' Will's face was set in grim lines as he remembered that bleak period. 'I'm a scientist. I understand about ocean currents, and protogyny among coral-reef fish, and sampling by random quadrats, but I wasn't well equipped to deal with divorce lawyers. It took me too long to get my own hot-shot lawyers and take the fight back...and by the time I did Nikki had changed tactics.'

Alice frowned. She didn't like the image of Will, bruised from the wreckage of his marriage, frustrated by lawyers and manipulated by Nikki. No wonder there were harsh lines on his face now. 'In what way?'

'She opted for emotional blackmail next,' he said, and, although he was clearly trying to keep his voice neutral, it was impossible to miss the underlying thread of bitterness. 'And very effective it was, too. Lily was already a toddler by then, and Nikki claimed it would be too unsettling for her to see me regularly. I wouldn't understand her needs the way Nikki did. It would distress Lily to go and stay somewhere strange. She didn't know who I was. I wouldn't know how to look after her properly. She needed to be in a familiar environment. It would be too disruptive for her to spend longer than a couple of hours with me. And so on and so on.'

'With the result that you became even more of a stranger to Lily?'

'Exactly. The few times I did manage to see Lily I was only able to take her out for a few hours, and frankly they weren't successful visits. I think Nikki was so paranoid about the possibility of me taking her away altogether that she'd transferred all her tension and suspicion to Lily. It's not surprising that she was nervous of me. As far as she was concerned, I was a stranger her mother didn't trust.'

He rubbed his face again, pushing his fingers back through his hair with a tired sigh. 'It wasn't just Nikki's fault. I didn't know how to reach Lily either. I wanted to tell Lily how much she meant to me, but I didn't know how, and I still don't. I've got no experience of being a father, and, now that I've got Lily all the time, I just feel inadequate. I either try too hard, or I get it completely wrong.'

He sounded so dispirited that Alice found herself reaching out to lay a comforting hand on his arm.

'You got it right tonight,' she told him.

She was burningly aware of his hard muscles beneath her fingers, and wished that she hadn't touched him. She had reached out instinctively, but now that her hand was on his arm it seemed suddenly a big deal, and she felt jolted, as if she had done something incredibly daring.

Which was ridiculous. It was only a matter of a hand on his forearm, after all. No reason to feel as if she had done the equivalent of clambering onto his lap, unbuttoning his shirt, pressing hot kisses up his throat …

Alice swallowed. She wasn't even touching his skin, for God's sake! Will was wearing a long-sleeved shirt rolled back at the wrist, but there was only a thin barrier of cotton between his skin and hers, and she was sure that she could feel his warmth and strength through the fine material anyway.

Horribly conscious of the way her body was thrumming in response, she made herself pull her hand away. She couldn't have been touching him for more than a few seconds, but her heart was beating so hard she was afraid Will would be able to hear it above the crescendo of the night insects.

In this light it was impossible to tell whether he had even registered her touch, and his voice sounded perfectly normal as he credited her with the small progress he had made with Lily.

'Thanks to you,' he said. 'The books were your idea.'

'But you were the one who read to her.' Sure that her cheeks were still burning with awareness, Alice was very grateful for the darkness that she hoped hid her expression as effectively as it did Will's.

'You're good with children,' he said abruptly. 'Somehow I never imagined that you would be.'

'I'm not really,' she confessed, glad that her voice seemed steadier now. 'I'm not usually that interested in them. But I like Lily.'

'You've never wanted children of your own?'

Alice thought about the years she had spent trying to find a man she could settle down and be happy with, a man she could build a family with, a man who would make her forget Will and all that she had walked away from. She had thought she had found him at last in Tony. They had talked about having children, when they were married, when the time was right. But sometimes the time was never right, and, even if it was, it wasn't always that easy. Look at Roger and Beth.

'You can't always have what you want,' she said in a low voice, and Will turned to her, wondering if she was thinking about Tony who she had loved so much, and thinking about how much he had wanted her for so long.

'No,' he agreed. 'Sometimes you can't.'

'It'll rain soon.' Will handed Alice a glass of fresh lime juice chinking with ice, and sat down next to her with a cold beer.

'I hope so.' Alice took the glass with a murmur of thanks and held it against her cheek, letting the condensation cool her skin. 'Mmm…that feels nice,' she told Will, who had to make himself look away from the sight of her, her eyes closed in pleasure as the condensation on the glass trickled down her throat and into her cleavage. It was dark on the verandah, but sometimes not dark enough.

'It's been so hot today,' she went on, languid with heat. 'I took Lily over to see Beth today so we could sit in the air-conditioning for a while.'

With her free hand, Alice lifted a few damp strands of hair that had fallen from their clip onto the back of her neck. 'The heat doesn't usually bother me, but for the last couple of days it's been suffocating. It's like trying to breathe through a scarf.'

'It's the pressure.' Will was dismayed at how hoarse his voice sounded. 'A good storm will clear the air.'

'I can't wait,' she sighed. 'There's no sign of any rain clouds, though. I've been looking at the horizon all day.'

'They'll be boiling up now,' said Will. 'Didn't you notice them at sunset? That's always a sign. It has to break soon.'

He wished that he was just talking meteorologically. A different kind of pressure had been building inexorably over the ten days since Alice had arrived, and Will was finding it harder and harder to ignore.

He had done his best to try and think of her simply as Lily's nanny, but it wasn't any good. She was resolutely Alice, impossible to ignore. It didn't matter if she was just sitting quietly next to him in the dark, or playing cards with Lily or laying the table. It was there in every turn of her head, every gesture of her hands, every sweep of her lashes.

Will struggled to remember how he had disliked her at Roger and Beth's party, but that tense, brittle, superficial Alice had somehow been whittled away by the heat, the sunlight and the warm breeze that riffled the lagoon and rustled through the coconut palms. He had to remind himself constantly that she hadn't really changed that much. She still wore that absurd collection of shoes. She flicked through magazines and talked about clothes, make-up and God knew what else, encouraging Lily to remember her life in London more than Will wanted. She still talked about the great career she was going to resume.

She was still going home.

He needed to keep that in mind, Will told himself at least once a day. She would only be there for another few weeks, and then she would be gone. He would have to start thinking about life without her all over again.

It alarmed him how easily they had slipped into a routine, and he was afraid that he was getting used to it. He left early for work, but for the first time in years found himself looking forward to going home at the end of the day. Alice and Lily were usually on the verandah, playing games or reading together, and he would often stand behind the screen door and watch them, unobserved for a while, disturbed by the intensity of pleasure the peaceful scene gave him. Sometimes he tried to tell himself he would have felt the same no matter who was with Lily, but he knew that he was fooling himself.

It wasn't just the fact that Lily was gradually settling down. It was Alice.

Every night when Lily was asleep, they would sit on the verandah, like now, and they would talk easily until one of them made an unthinking comment that reminded them of the past and all they had meant to each other. And when that happened, the tension a routine kept successfully at bay most of the time would trickle back into the atmosphere, stretching the silence uncomfortably until one or other of them made an excuse and went to bed.

Will had hoped that the weekend would break that pattern, and things had certainly been different since then. He just wasn't convinced that it was for the better.

On the Saturday he had taken the two of them out to the reef in the project's tin boat. Half-submerged in a life jacket that was really too big for her, Lily had clutched onto the wooden seat. Her face had been shaded by a floppy cotton hat, but, sitting opposite her at the helm, Will could peer under the brim and see that her expression was an odd mixture of excitement and trepidation. She'd looked as if she wanted to be thrilled, but didn't quite dare to let herself go.

'Would you like to drive the boat?' he asked her, and her eyes widened.

'I don't know how.'

'I'll show you.'

Will held out his hand, and after a moment, with some encouragement from Alice, she took it and let herself be handed carefully across to stand between his knees. He showed her how to hold the tiller, and kept her steady, guiding the boat unobtrusively from behind. Lily's small body was tense with concentration, and it was hard to know whether she was terrified or loving it.

Over her head, he could see Alice, straight-backed as ever on the narrow seat, holding her hat onto her head. Her eyes were hidden by sunglasses, but when she met his gaze she smiled and nodded at Lily. 'She's smiling,' she mouthed, as if she knew what he most wanted to hear, and Will felt his heart swell with happiness.

The sun glittered on the water, bouncing off every surface and throwing dazzling patterns over Alice's face as the little boat bounced over the waves. Everything seemed extraordinarily clear, suddenly: the breeze in his hair, the tang of the sea in his lungs, his daughter smiling as she leant into him… And Alice, contrary, prickly, unforgettable Alice. At that moment, Will felt something close to vertigo, a spinning sensation as if he were teetering on the edge of a cliff, and he had to jerk his gaze away before he did something stupid like telling her that he loved her still.

Bad idea.

It had been a happy day, though. They pulled the boat onto a tiny coral island, where they could wade into the warm water and watch the fish dart around their ankles, flashing silver in the sunlight. Will taught Lily how to snorkel while Alice sat under a solitary leaning palm and unpacked the picnic they had brought.

Afterwards, Lily dozed off in the shade, and Will watched Alice wandering along the shore. The set of her head on that straight spine was so familiar it made Will ache. Her loose white-linen trousers were rolled up to her knees, her face shadowed by the brim of her hat, a pair of delicate sandals dangling from her hand.

'You won't need shoes,' Will had said when they'd got into the boat that morning, but Alice had refused to leave them behind in the car.

'I feel more comfortable with shoes on,' she had said. 'You never know when you're going to need them to run away.'

'You won't be able to run very far on the reef,' Will had pointed out, but she'd only lifted her chin at him.

'I'm keeping them on.'

Alice would always want an escape-route planned, he realised as he watched her pause and look out across the translucent green of the lagoon to where the deep blue of the Indian Ocean frothed in bright white against the far reef. She would always want to be able to run away, just as she had run away from him before.

She wouldn't be here now if she didn't have that ticket home, Will remembered. It would be foolish to let himself hope that she might stay. She wasn't going to, and he had to accept that now. Consciously steadying his heart, he made himself think coolly and practically. He mustn't be seduced by the sea and the sunlight and Alice's smile. Sure, he could enjoy today, but he wouldn't expect it to last. There were no for evers where Alice was concerned.

When Lily woke up, she ran instantly down to join Alice at the water's edge. Will watched them both, and tried not to mind that his daughter so obviously preferred Alice's company to his. Tried not to worry, too, how she would manage when Alice was gone.

He could see them bending down to examine things they found on the beach. Alice was crouching down, turning something in her hand and showing it to Lily, who took it and studied it carefully.

And then it happened.

'Daddy!' she cried, running up the beach towards him. 'Daddy, look!'

It was a cowrie shell, small but perfect, with an unusual leopard pattern on its back, but Will hardly noticed it. He was overwhelmed by the fact that Lily had run to him, had called him Daddy, had wanted him to share in her pleasure, and his throat closed so tightly with emotion that it was hard to speak.

'This is a great shell,' he managed. 'It's an unusual one, too. You were very clever to find it.'

'Alice found it,' Lily admitted with reluctant honesty, and Will looked up to see Alice, who had followed more slowly up the beach. Their eyes met over Lily's dark head, and she smiled at him, knowing exactly what Lily's excited dash up the beach had meant to him.

Will smiled back, pushing the future firmly out of his mind. He knew the day wouldn't last for ever, but right then, with Lily's intent face, the feel of the shell in his palm, and Alice smiling at him, it was enough.

CHAPTER EIGHT

WILL was thinking about that day out on the reef as he sat on the verandah with Alice and the hot air creaked with the pressure of the oncoming storm. He had done his best to keep his distance from her since then.

Again and again, he had reminded himself that she would be leaving soon and that there was no point in noticing the curve of her mouth, or the line of her throat, or the sheen of her skin in the crushing heat. No point in remembering how she felt, how she tasted. No point in thinking about how sweet and exciting and *right* it had felt to make love to her.

Not doing any of that was definitely the sensible thing to do. But it was hard.

'Listen!' Alice held up a hand suddenly, startling Will out of his thoughts.

'What is it? Is it Lily?' he asked, instantly anxious in case he had missed a cry.

'It's the insects.'

Will looked at her puzzled. 'What insects?'

'Exactly. They've stopped.'

And, sure enough, the deafening rasp, scratch and shrill of the insects, that was such a familiar backdrop to the evenings here that Will barely heard it any more, had paused and in its place was an uncanny silence.

The next instant there was a rip of lightning in the distance, an almighty crack of thunder overhead, and a deluge of rain came crashing down onto the roof. One second there had been the hot, heavy, *waiting* silence, the next there was nothing but sound and fury and the pounding, thundering, hammering rain. It fell not in drops but as a solid mass, bouncing back in the air as it hit solid ground, and overwhelming the gutters so that it simply cascaded in a sheet over the edge of the verandah.

Alice laughed with sheer delight. 'I *love* it when it rains like this!' she shouted to Will, but it was doubtful that he could hear her over the deafening roar of the rain.

Caught up in the elemental excitement of the downpour, she jumped to her feet. The sheer power of it was awe-inspiring, almost frightening, but exhilarating at the same time. Alice could feel the raw energy of it surging around the verandah, pushing and pulling at her, making her blood pound.

Normally she hated feeling so out of control, but a tropical downpour was different. She knew it wouldn't last very long, but while it did she could feel wild and reckless, the way she would never allow herself to be the rest of the time.

She looked at Will, who had got to his feet too, moved by the same restless excitement generated by the breaking of the pressure that had been pressing down on them for the last few days. He was watching the rain, his intelligent face alive with interest, the stern mouth curling upwards into an almost-smile, and, as her eyes rested on him, Alice was gripped by a hunger to touch him once more, to feel his hard hands against her skin, to abandon herself to the electricity in the air.

Instinctively, she took a step towards him, just at the moment when the force of the rain finally succeeded in dislodging part of the roof and poured through a hole directly onto her head. If Alice had stayed where she was, the water would have splashed harmlessly onto the verandah, but as it was she was drenched instantly.

It felt as if someone had tipped a bucket over her, and she gasped with the shock of it before she started to laugh again. It was like standing under a waterfall, the water cool and indescribably refreshing after the suffocating heat, and as it was too late to get dry Alice closed her eyes and tipped her face up to the cascading water.

In seconds her dress was clinging to her, and her shoes—her favourite jewelled kitten-heels—were probably ruined, but right then Alice didn't care. Pulling the clip from her hair, she shook it free and let the rain plaster it to her head as it ran in rivulets over her face and down her throat.

Will had been unable not to laugh at the sight of her ambushed by the leak in the roof, but as he watched her close her eyes and turn her face up to the water, as he watched the fine fabric of her dress stick to her breasts and hips, as he watched the rain sliding over skin, his smile faded at the extraordinary sensuality of the scene, and his body tightened.

As if sensing his reaction, Alice opened her eyes. Her lashes were wet and spiky, and she had to blink against the water running over her face, but her gaze was dark and steady.

There was no need for either of them to say anything. They both knew that the careful defences they had built over the last couple of weeks were no match for the downpour. For tonight, the rules, their hopes and their fears, meant nothing. There was only the two of them, the crackle of electricity, and the drumming rain. When Will reached for her, Alice reached out at the same time and tugged him under the rain still pouring through the hole in the roof.

They kissed with the water spilling around them, trickling

from his skin onto hers, and from hers to his, their bodies pressing so close that it couldn't find a way between them. They kissed and kissed and kissed again, hard, hungry kisses that fed on the power of the downpour and on the spiralling excitement that spun and surged as they touched each other with increasing urgency. Their hands moved instinctively over each other, clutching, clasping, sliding, shifting, finding long-remembered secret places, rediscovering the feel and the taste and the touch of each other.

'Will…' Alice pressed her lips to his throat in fevered kisses, revelling in the feel of his body, in the wonderful, familiar smell of his skin, arching and shuddering with pleasure at the touch of his hands, the taste of his mouth, How could she have told herself that she had forgotten how it felt? 'Will…' she gasped, inarticulate with need.

'What?' he murmured raggedly against her throat. They might as well have been naked already. Their clothes were plastered to their wet bodies, and should have felt cold and clammy, but the heat of their beating blood was keeping them warm. Will wouldn't have been surprised to see steam rising.

Alice didn't know what she wanted to say, didn't know how to tell him how she felt. Her mind was reeling with pleasure, and all she could think about was the clamour of her body, the desire that was running rampant, unstoppable, out of control…

'Tell me what you want, Alice,' Will whispered, and then lifted his head so that he could look down into her face, his own streaked with water now too.

'I don't know,' said Alice helplessly.

But she did know. She wanted him. She wanted more of him, all of him. She wanted him closer, harder, inside her. She wanted him completely—but the very strength of her need was beginning to alarm her, while a small voice of reason inside her was insinuating itself into the wild recklessness that had gripped her, telling her to be careful, reminding her about the past and the future, about the risk of abandoning herself utterly to the moment.

Oh, how she wanted to, though!

'I want …' she began unsteadily, and then swallowed. 'I want to pretend that this is all there is,' she told him at last.

'This *is* all there is,' said Will. 'This is all that matters.' And, taking her hand, he led her inside and out of the rain.

Alice lay next to Will and let her pounding blood slow, her breathing steady. Her entire body was still thrumming with satisfaction, and she felt heady and boneless. It was impossible to regret what had happened, even now the wildness and the excitement of the night had dissipated. Their bodies had remembered each other with a heart-stopping clarity, their senses snarling and tangling and tantalizing, surrendering together to the soaring rhythm of love until they'd shattered with release.

It had been wonderful. She could hardly pretend otherwise when the glory was still beating through her veins and shimmering out to the very tips of her toes. And it hadn't been wrong. They were both single, both free, both responsible adults. No one was going to be hurt by what they had done.

But…

Why did it feel as if that huge 'but' was hovering, just waiting to be acknowledged?

Alice turned her head on the pillow to look at Will. He was lying on his back, and she could see his chest rising and falling unevenly as his breathing returned to normal. Outside it was still raining, although not with the ferocity of earlier, and the sound was comforting rather than exhilarating. If it had rained like this earlier, would they have still ended up in bed?

Perhaps. Probably, even. If Alice was going to be honest, she would have to admit that she had been finding it harder and harder to resist the tug of attraction as the days had passed. She'd only had to look at him reading a story to Lily, or at the helm of the boat, his hair lifting in the breeze and his eyes full of sunlight, or lifting a glass to his lips, and her mouth would dry and her stomach would clench. She could say what she liked about being friends, but the old chemistry was still there, and they both knew it.

So, yes, perhaps tonight had been inevitable, but what now? They couldn't just go back to the careful way they had been before, but what other choice did they have? A tiny sigh escaped Alice as she stared up at the ceiling. She should have made it clear to Will that it had just been the storm, and that she wasn't expecting anything to change just because they had made love tonight.

'You know, you don't need to fret.' Will's voice came unexpectedly out of the darkness, making Alice jump.

'I'm not fretting!'

'Yes, you are.' Will rolled so that he could prop himself up on one elbow and look down at where she lay, her bare skin luminous in the faint light and her hair still wet and tangled on the pillow. 'I know you, Alice. You're planning your escape route right now.'

'What do you mean?' she asked uneasily.

'You always look for a way out before there's any chance that you might end up committing yourself.'

'That's rubbish!' she scoffed, but not quite as convincingly as she would have liked. Will certainly wasn't fooled.

'Is it? Don't try and tell me you weren't lying there trying to work out how soon you could tell me that you only wanted this for tonight, that it didn't mean anything to you and that it wasn't meant to be for ever.'

'What did you think it was?' retorted Alice, glad that he had found the words for her.

'I wasn't thinking at all.' Will's wry smile gleamed in the darkness. 'I can't say I regret it, though. It wasn't something either of us planned, but I think it was something we both wanted—or are you going to deny that?'

'No, I'm not going to deny it,' she said in a low voice. 'There's always been a special chemistry between us.'

'I know that. You don't need to worry, Alice.' Will reached out and lifted a lock of her wet hair, rubbing it gently between his fingers. 'You don't need to explain or make excuses. I know you're leaving, so you don't have to think of a way out. Let's just leave tonight as an itch that we both scratched.'

It ought to have made Alice feel better, but somehow it didn't. She knew that Will was right, and that he was giving her exactly what she needed, but she didn't want to be an *itch*.

Sitting up, she pushed her damp hair away from her face and reached down for the sheet that had slipped unheeded to the floor much earlier. 'Is that it?' she asked almost sharply as she wrapped it around her.

'What more can it be?'

'Well…there's still three weeks or so until I go,' she found herself saying.

There was a pause. 'What are you suggesting, Alice?' he asked, and it was impossible to tell from his voice what he was thinking. 'That we keep scratching that itch?'

'If that's how you want to think of it.' Alice bit her lip and pulled more of the sheet onto the bed. 'You were right about the way out. There's no point in pretending that I'm not leaving in three weeks' time, so I'm not making any promises. I wouldn't want you to think that I'm talking about for ever.'

'Don't worry,' said Will, at his most dry. 'I learnt a long time ago never to think of you and for ever in the same sentence.'

'Then, if we both know that, why not make the most of it?'

Part of Alice was rearing up in alarm at her insistence, and warning her that nothing good could come of getting involved with Will again. It was all very well to talk about scratching an itch, but, once you had given in to the need, it was almost impossible to stop. It was madness to think that she could sleep with him for three weeks and then calmly walk away. Better to leave things as they were, as Will himself had suggested, and treat tonight as a one-off. She had a nice house and a life to go back to in London. That was enough, wasn't it?

But another, more reckless, part had her in its grip tonight. Why not? it was asking. How long was it since she had felt that gorgeously, fabulously good, that relaxed, that *sexy*? What was the point of not doing it again, when they had another three weeks or more to get through? They both knew where they were. They had no expectations of each other. And it had been great. Did she *really* want that to be the last time?

No, she didn't.

'It would be fun,' she coaxed, realising at that moment that it was a very long time since she had let herself simply have fun. Ten years, in fact.

Will was silent for a moment. 'I don't want to fall in love with you again, Alice,' he said.

'We won't fall in love,' she said. 'We've been there, and we know it doesn't work. That doesn't mean we can't have a good time together.'

'So you just want me for my body?' said Will, but Alice was sure she could hear a smile in his voice.

'We-el…' She let the sheet fall and slid back down beside him, letting her hand drift tantalisingly over his flat stomach, and scratching him very, very lightly with her nails. 'If the itch is there, we might as well scratch it, don't you think?'

The downward drift of her fingers was making it hard for

Will to think clearly. 'So we'll have the next few weeks and then say goodbye?' he managed.

Alice's hand paused for just a second. 'Then we'll say goodbye,' she agreed.

Will knew that he was probably making a mistake but right then, with her fingers teasing him and her lips against his throat, and her body warm and soft and close, he didn't care. Moving swiftly, he pinned her beneath him and put his hands on either side of her face. 'All right,' he said as he bent to kiss her. 'Three weeks. Let's make them good ones.'

It didn't work, of course. They had about a week when they both resolutely closed their minds to the future, and thought only about the days with Lily and the long, hot nights together. It was easy to fall into their old ways, talking, laughing, arguing, making love… And inevitable, Will thought, that he should start wishing that it could go on for ever.

Knowing that, it made him increasingly tense and irritable. He was angry with Alice for her dogged refusal to consider taking a risk on the unknown, angrier with himself for agreeing to the one situation that he had most wanted to avoid.

Because of *course* he had fallen in love with Alice again. The truth was that he had probably never fallen out of love with her, and it wasn't helping matters to have her there whenever he went home, as combative, challenging and stimulating as ever, as warm and responsive every night. Every time Will looked at her, his heart seemed to stop, and the knowledge that he would have to let her go gnawed relentlessly at him.

Three weeks, that was all they had. After the heady delight of that first week, Will did his best to distance himself from her. But how could he when she was there in his bed, when she lay warm against him all night, and her very nearness made his head reel?

Alice sensed his withdrawal, even understood it. It had been a wonderful week, but slowly the sensible side of her was regaining its natural ascendancy. Ah-ha! it cried. Told you you'd regret it! Look what a mess you've got yourself into *now*!

The three-week deadline changed her whole sense of time. Sometimes it seemed to rush forward with dizzying speed, making her panic, and at others it slowed to a lethargic trickle that made it impossible to imagine the future. Alice tried to focus on going home, but her life in England seemed increasingly unreal.

She had expected to start feeling bored by now, to start yearning for shops, cinemas, bars and the gossip and pressure of a proper job, but it hadn't happened yet. She tried to make herself miss them, but how could she think about London when Lily chattered as she swung on her hand, and the lagoon glittered behind the coconut palms, and Will closed the bedroom door every night with a smile?

The arrival of Lily's trunk only underlined how far she was from home. Having made such a fuss about Will not bringing his daughter's things with him, Alice had to admit that none of the clothes were suitable for a tropical island. There were surprisingly few books, and a lot of very expensive and hardly-used toys, none of which seemed to interest Lily very much.

She had to find *some* way of detaching herself from life here, Alice thought with increasing desperation. It was too comfortable, too intimate, with just the three of them. She needed to get out and meet more people, make her life bigger again so that when she left there wouldn't be an aching gap where Will and Lily had been. Deep down, Alice was afraid that she might have left it too late for that, but at least it was a plan.

When Will told her that he and his team were preparing for an open day at the project headquarters that Friday, Alice leapt at the opportunity.

'Can we come?'

'To the open day?' Will looked taken aback at the idea.

'Why not? It would be a chance for Lily to see what you do all day.'

'I'm not sure it'll be of any interest to a child. We've got a government minister coming, but it's really about trying to involve the local community in the project, especially the fishermen, and getting them to understand what we're trying to do.'

'Why don't you lay something on for all the children?' said Alice. 'They're part of the community too, and if you get them on board now it'll make things much easier in the future. You could lay on little trips for them,' she went on, warming to her theme. 'Or have a competition with little prizes…you know, they have to find out information as they go round and answer questions, or find something, like a treasure hunt.'

'I suppose we *could* do something for the children,' said Will slowly.

'It'll be good for Lily to start meeting other children before she goes to school, too,' Alice pointed out.

Impressed by her enthusiasm, Will considered. 'Could you run some activities for the children?'

'Me?'

'It was your idea.'

'But I don't know anything about marine ecology!'

'We can give you the information you need. It's putting it into an appealing format we'd find more difficult, even if we had the time to think about it, which we don't. We've got enough to do setting up displays for the open day as it is, and we're running short of time.'

So Alice and Lily found themselves at the project headquarters. The building was simply, even spartanly, furnished, but everything was very well organised. It was clear that all the money was spent on expertise and research equipment—

no surprise with Will in charge. The whole project had his stamp on it; high quality, integrity, and absolutely no frills.

Will showed them round and introduced them to various members of the team, all of whom welcomed Lily kindly and eyed Alice with unmistakable curiosity. He had introduced her simply as 'a friend', and it was obvious that they were all wondering just how close a friend she was. Alice found herself unaccountably miffed that he wouldn't acknowledge a closer relationship, because clearly they *were* more than friends. They were lovers.

Desire shivered through her at the thought of the nights they spent together. She would never guess it to look at Will now. He was dressed casually but with characteristic neatness in shorts and a short-sleeved shirt, and his face was absorbed as he discussed some obscure issue to do with phytoplankton, whatever that was, with a bearded marine biologist. Looking at the back of those long, straight legs, Alice felt quite weak with the knowledge of how they felt against hers, of what it was like to kiss the nape of his neck and slide her arms around that lean, hard body.

'Shall we go and look at the lab?' Will turned to find Alice staring at him, and she gulped and jerked her gaze away.

'Fine,' she said brightly. 'Lead on!'

In spite of herself, Alice was impressed by what she saw. She hadn't realised quite what a major project it was, and she remembered how glibly she had suggested to Will that he give up his career and find another job in London. It seemed an absurd idea now. For it was clear that he was key to the project's success. The staff made no secret of how much they admired him, and Alice could see why. He didn't raise his voice, or show off or patronise anyone, but somehow he was at the centre of everything. She saw a young diver glow at Will's quiet word of congratulation, and a secretary nod with enthusiasm at one of his suggestions. This was Will in his element, intelligent, focused, completely assured about who he was, what he was doing and why he was doing it.

It was very different from her own world of work where status symbols were so important, and how you looked and talked sometimes mattered more than what you actually did. Alice couldn't help comparing Will with Tony, who was always so careful of his appearance and so competitive. Tony would talk himself up in meetings, never missing an opportunity to tell everyone how dynamic and successful he was, and even at home he hadn't been able to wait to tell Alice how well he had performed in a meeting or how much better his results had been than any of his colleagues.

Alice's own drive was less for success in itself than for the security it brought, but she sensed that the team had some reservations about her, and she supposed she did look a bit out of place in her narrow skirt, sleeveless top and high peep-toe shoes with their pretty candy stripes. Alice told herself that she didn't care what they thought of her, and threw herself into the challenge of taking what she had learnt and making it fun and accessible for children.

Will found her a desk, and she and Lily spent the rest of the day happily playing around with ideas and thinking up simple questions that a child like Lily could answer by looking at the various display boards that were being prepared. Will disappeared out to the reef, and Alice found it easier to settle once he had gone. She chatted to the two locally employed secretaries, who adored Will, and were obviously longing to know more about his relationship with Alice but were too polite to ask outright.

'I'm just helping out with Lily until the new nanny arrives,' she told them, since there didn't seem any reason to keep it a big secret. 'I'm going home soon.'

Perhaps, if she said it enough, it would start to seem real.

She liked the atmosphere in the office. It made her realise how much she missed having to think and be part of a team, a train of thought Alice was keen to encourage in herself. Because missing that meant that she was missing work, which meant, obviously, that she was looking forward to going back to London and applying for what she was determined would be the job of her dreams.

Together with Lily, she came up with a competition and a treasure hunt, and begged the use of a computer to draft fun forms for the children to fill in. Then she rang Roger and cajoled him into sponsoring prizes for everyone who took part, as she was pretty sure Will wouldn't approve of using his precious budget to finance frivolities.

'It'll be good PR for your company,' she told him.

'A bunch of children in fishing villages aren't exactly our target market,' said Roger, but he was happy to humour her, and the cost was negligible for a company like his in any case.

It wasn't long before Alice was coming up with other ideas. She told Will about Roger's offer as they drove home at the end of the day. 'Why don't you make this an opportunity to get more sponsorship?'

'I haven't got time for schmoozing,' said Will, changing gear irritably. He was tense after a day spent trying to ignore Alice's warm, vibrant presence in the office. It had been bad enough trying to concentrate on work before, when his senses had still been reeling with memories of the night before, but today had been virtually impossible. Wherever he looked, there she was, sitting on the edge of the desk, swinging those ridiculous shoes, chatting to the secretaries, bending over pieces of paper with Lily, their faces intent, studying the display boards …

Her questions had been intelligent, and she had made some

acute observations, which shouldn't have surprised him. Nobody could ever have accused Alice of being stupid, and he could see that, although the team had been wary of her initially, they had all been impressed by her ideas in the end. She had flair, Will had to admit. It was hard to put his finger on it, but there was a certain stylishness about everything she did, and there was no doubt that she had already made a huge contribution to the plans for the open day.

So he ought to be feeling pleased with her, not edgy and cross. Grateful as he was for her ideas, he wished that she had stayed at home. Now, when she had gone, he wouldn't even be able to go to the office without memories of her waiting to ambush him.

'You wouldn't need to spend any extra time,' said Alice, taking out her clip and wedging it between her teeth as she shook out her hair. 'You're having the open day anyway,' she pointed out, rather muffled through the clip. 'Why not invite businesses along at the same time and show them what you're doing?'

Twisting her hair back up with one hand, she took the clip from her teeth and deftly secured it into place. 'You're the one who said how important the protection of the reef is to the economy. That makes it of interest to companies who operate here, local and international, and I'm sure lots of them would be interested in sponsoring you. Jumping on the environmental awareness bandwagon makes good PR for them.'

'The point of the open day is to keep government support and to involve the local communities,' Will grumbled. 'You're wanting to turn it into a jamboree.'

'Nonsense,' said Alice briskly. 'All you need to do is lay on a few more drinks, and it'll be worth it if you get some extra money for the project, won't it? Besides,' she said, turning to wink at Lily in the back seat, 'if we make it a party, it'll be a chance for Lily and I to dress up.'

Lily brightened. 'Can I wear my pink shoes?'

'You can,' said Alice. 'And I'll wear my shoes with the bows. What do you think?' she asked, ignoring Will's snort.

'I like them.'

'I'm so glad we've got the footwear sorted out,' said Will sarcastically as they turned into their road. 'Now there's nothing else to worry about!'

Although, as it turned out, there was.

An email from the agency in London was waiting for him when he went into the office the next day. Will sat at his desk and stared at the screen. They had found an excellent candidate, the email informed him. An experienced nanny, mature and sensible, Helen would be able to fly out to St Bonaventure as soon as required. Would he please read the attached CV and their comments on Helen's interview and let them know as soon as possible if he wished to offer her the post.

Will lifted his eyes from the screen. Through the glass wall of his office he could see Alice on the phone. She had taken responsibility for the refreshments, and her face was animated as she talked, one hand holding the phone to her ear, the other gesticulating as if the person on the other end could see her.

When she had gone, he wouldn't be able to look at that phone without imagining her as she was now. He wouldn't be able to sit on the verandah in the evening without feeling her beside him, talking, stretching, waving her arms around, laughing, arguing, her face vivid in the darkness. He wouldn't be able to lie in bed without remembering her kisses, her softness and her warmth, the silken fire of her.

When she had gone, there would be an aching, empty void wherever she had been.

'I need to talk to you,' he said to her that night after they had put Lily to bed.

'That sounds serious,' said Alice lightly. 'Had we better sit down?'

So they sat in their accustomed places on the verandah, and Will tried to marshal the churning thoughts that had been occupying him all day. He hadn't been able to talk to her at the office, and he didn't want to say anything in front of Lily. He'd thought he'd decided what he was going to say, but now that he was here his careful arguments seemed to have vanished.

'What is it?' asked Alice after a while.

'I had an email today from the agency in London. They've found a nanny who sounds very suitable and she can come out next week if I want.'

Alice sat very still. Funny, she had known this was going to happen—it was what she had insisted should happen—but, now that the moment was here, she was completely unprepared. Everything had worked out perfectly. A nanny was available. Lily was going to school soon, and there would be someone to look after her when Will wasn't there. She could go home.

It was just what she wanted.

So why did her heart feel as if it had turned to a stone in her chest?

'I see,' she said, and from somewhere produced a smile. 'Well, that's good news. What's her name?'

'Helen.'

Helen would soon be sitting here with him. Helen would meet Lily from school and kiss her knees when she fell down. Helen would be waiting for him when he got home in the evening.

Is she pretty? Alice wanted to ask. Is she young? Will you fall in love with her?

'When's she coming?' she asked instead.

'I haven't replied yet,' said Will. 'I wanted to talk to you first.' He hesitated. 'I wanted to ask if you would stay.'

CHAPTER NINE

'STAY?' Alice echoed blankly.

'Yes, stay. Lily loves you, she'll miss you. And I'll miss you too,' Will admitted honestly. 'I'm not asking you to stay for ever, Alice. I know how you feel about commitment, but the last couple of weeks have been good, haven't they?'

'Yes,' she said, unable to deny it.

'Then why not carry on as we are?' he said, uncomfortably aware of the undercurrent of urgency, even desperation, in his voice. He cleared his throat and tried to sound more normal. 'You told me yourself that your engagement had fallen through and that you didn't have a job at the moment. What have you got to go home to?'

'My home,' said Alice a little defensively. 'My life.'

'You could have a home and a life here.'

'For how long?' she asked. 'I can't pretend I haven't enjoyed the last few weeks, Will. It's been a special time, but special times don't last.'

'They don't if you don't give them a chance,' said Will.

She bit her lip. The thought of saying goodbye to him and Lily tore at her, but he was asking her to give up her whole life, and for what?

'How can they last?' she said. 'Lily will be going to school soon, and what would I do then? You've got an absorbing job, Sara looks after the house. There's no place for me here, Will. How long would it be before I get bored, and everything that's made this such a wonderful time disappears?'

'You could find something to do,' said Will. 'Look at how you've taken over with the open day. Someone with your organisational skills will always find a job.'

'I might find some temporary or voluntary work, but that's not what I want. I've got a career, and the longer I stay away from it the more difficult it will be to go back to it. I've worked hard to get to this stage,' she told him. 'I can't just chuck it all in now on the basis of a few happy weeks.'

'At least you admit you have been happy,' said Will with an unmistakable thread of bitterness. 'Are you going to be happy in London? No, don't answer that,' he said as Alice hesitated. 'You've always put your career before your happiness, haven't you?'

'At least I can rely on my career to give me satisfaction and security,' she retorted. 'You can't rely on being happy.'

'But if you don't take the risk you'll never know how happy you could be.'

Alice sighed and pushed a stray strand of hair behind her ear. 'We've been through all this before, Will,' she reminded him. 'You've got your career, I've got mine, and they don't fit together. We still want different things from life.'

'So you won't stay?' he asked heavily. 'Not even for a while?'

She swallowed. 'No.' And then, when he said nothing, 'Surely you can see that the longer I stay, the harder it's going to be to say goodbye? It's going to come to goodbye sometime, and I think it would be easier for both of us to do it sooner rather than later.'

'All right,' said Will after a moment, his voice empty of expression now. 'I'll email the agency tomorrow and get them to send Helen out as soon as possible.'

Alice didn't reply. She sat unmoving in her chair, paralysed by the weight of the decision she had made. It was the right one, she knew, but that didn't stop her feeling leaden inside, and her throat was so tight she couldn't have spoken if she'd tried.

Beside her, Will looked out at the darkness, his jaw clenched with disappointment and a kind of rage for allowing himself to even hope that she would say yes when he must have known that she would say no.

The insects shrilled into the silence, and for a while there was nothing else but the sound of the ocean beyond the reef and the sadness of knowing that the love and the joy they had shared wasn't going to be enough.

At last, Will drew a long breath and got to his feet. 'Come on,' he said, holding a hand down to her. 'Let's go to bed.'

He stopped as he saw her expression rinsed with surprise, and the hand which he had reached out so instinctively fell to his side. 'Would you rather not?'

'No, it's not that,' said Alice, faltering. 'It's just...I didn't think *you* would want to.'

'We've still got a week left,' he said. 'You were the one who said that we should make the most of the time we had.'

'Yes.' Alice got up almost stiffly, overwhelmed by the relief that had rushed through her when she'd realised that Will wasn't going to reject her. She wouldn't have blamed him if he had, but the thought that she would never again lie in his arms had been a bitter one. Reaching out, she took his hand deliberately. 'Yes, I did.'

They didn't say a word to each other, but there was a desperation and a poignancy to their love-making that wrenched Alice's heart. There was no need to speak when every kiss, every touch, said more than words ever could how much they were going to miss each other.

By tacit agreement, they both threw themselves into the preparations for the open day. Anything was better than thinking about how they were going to say goodbye.

On Friday morning, Will sat impatiently in the car, waiting for Alice and Lily to appear. He had done his best to talk himself into believing that Alice's departure was for the best. She had worked really hard on the open day, but she didn't really fit in here, he reminded himself constantly. She had been right. There would be nothing for her to do on St Bonaventure, and she would soon get bored and restless. Look how little time it had taken for her to get fed up with staying with Beth. Far better for her to go now than to hang around until her frustration soured everything.

He should never have asked her to stay, Will told himself, drumming his fingers on the steering wheel and glancing at his watch for the umpteenth time. Alice had a pattern of running away at the first suggestion of commitment. She had always done it, and she always would. For someone with such forceful opinions, she was pathetic when it came to taking risks.

Will was conscious of the growing resentment inside him, which he fed deliberately because it was easier to be angry with Alice than to contemplate life when she was gone. Why had she had to come and upset everything? She could have stayed with Roger and Beth. They could have met a couple of times for some polite conversation and everything would have been fine. But no! She'd had to come and live with them. She had turned his world upside down all over again. She had made him fall in love with her all over again, and, now that she had made sure that she was right at the centre of his life and Lily's, she was going to leave them both feeling desolate.

Now the tension between them was worse than ever. They

hardly talked about anything except the open day. The only way they could communicate was in bed, where they made love with a fierceness and an intensity that left them both shattered. Will didn't know whether it making things better or worse. He just knew that his stomach felt as if a heavy stone were lodged inside it.

If nothing else, the delay allowed an outlet for his feelings. He leant on the horn. 'If you're not ready in two minutes, you can get a taxi,' he shouted. 'I've got to go.'

'We're coming!'

Alice and Lily came hurrying down the steps from the front door. Alice was holding Lily's hand and had a straw hat in the other. Will didn't know whether it was deliberate or not, but she was wearing the green dress she had worn at the party when he had first seen her again. She even had the same silly shoes on. It was almost as if she was making an effort to revert to the brittle, superficial person she had seemed then.

His daughter looked charming in a floppy hat, pink shoes, and a straight pink shift that Will didn't recall seeing before.

'New dress?' he asked, cocking an eye over his shoulder as she clambered into the back seat and Alice helped her fix her seat belt.

'Alice bought it for me.'

'A goodbye present,' Alice explained, getting in beside Will and settling herself with much smoothing and twitching of her skirt. 'I thought it was time to get her used to the idea of me going,' she added in an undertone as Will let out the clutch.

Big of her, thought Will sourly, resenting the way she seemed to treat the matter so practically.

'I don't want her to go,' said Lily, whose hearing was better than Alice had imagined.

Now look at the mess Alice had left him in. It was all very well for Alice, swanning back to her oh-so-important career in London, but he was going to be left trying to find a way to comfort a desolate daughter, and he had know idea how he was going to do it.

'Alice has to go home,' he said. 'I'm sure you'll like Helen. She sounds nice.'

Lily's bottom lip stuck out. 'I don't want Helen. I want Alice.'

'I'm not going yet,' Alice interrupted, determinedly bright. 'So let's all enjoy today.'

She might be able to enjoy it, Will thought darkly, but he couldn't. The only advantage was that he was too busy to think much. The open day proved to be a surprisingly popular event and, once the government minister's tour was out of the way, a steady stream of curious visitors came in to look around and find out what the project was all about and how it would affect them. Fishermen mixed with the expatriate crowd Alice had persuaded to come with a view to drumming up some financial support, and between them all ran what seemed like hordes of children who had got a whiff of the prizes. Alice's competition was a huge success, and even some of the adults tried it for fun.

It was a hot day, but Alice was cool and elegant at the centre of it all. It was hard to believe that this was the same woman who had rolled laughing with him in bed, her hair tickling his chest and her mouth curving against his skin, and his heart twisted as he watched her.

She seemed to be everywhere, organizing children, making sure people had drinks, smiling and talking, working unobtrusively to make the day a success. He couldn't help thinking that it would be easier for him if she were being selfish and false. As it was, her every move seemed designed to underline how much he would miss her when she was gone.

And how little she herself cared.

Alice was not, in fact, enjoying the day as much as Will

thought. It was a huge effort to keep the smile fixed to her face, especially when she kept catching glimpses of Will between the crowds. He was dressed rather more smartly today in honour of the minister, but she noticed that he talked to the fishermen in exactly the same way as he talked to the politician.

He'd told her that he only had the rudiments of the local language which he had picked up on previous trips, but he seemed to Alice to be able to communicate perfectly well, laughing and joking with the locals or explaining the project's objectives. She only had to look at how people reacted to him to know that he was able to do that clearly and without being condescending or patronising.

Studying him through the milling crowds, Alice was struck anew by the cool self-containment that set him apart from the others, and she was engulfed suddenly in a giddying thrill of pride and possession that she was the only one there who knew how the muscles flexed when she ran her palms over his back, who knew the taste of his skin, how warm and sure his hands felt.

Her breath shortened as she watched him, and her mouth was dry, and for the umpteenth time since that awful night on the verandah she dithered. Stay, he had asked her, and she had said no. Was she making a terrible mistake? Sometimes, like now, it felt as if saying goodbye would be the hardest thing she had ever done. And why do it if she didn't need to?

But, if today proved anything, it was that Will's career was as important to him as hers was to her. His marine research was an integral part of him, and she clung to her work as the one thing she had ever been able to feel sure of. She loved Will, Alice realised sadly. She just couldn't be sure whether she loved him enough to give up everything else that mattered to her, and, unless she *was* sure, it would be better for her to go home.

'Alice!'

Startled out of her gloomy thoughts, Alice turned to see Roger and Beth advancing on her, both smiling broadly, and quickly she fixed her own smile back into place.

'It's lovely to see you,' she said, hugging first one then the other. 'Thank you for coming—and for all those prizes, Roger! They've been a huge success with the children.'

'Where's Will?'

Alice didn't even have to look. She was always aware of where he was and what he was doing. 'Over there,' she said, indicating to where Will stood talking to a group of fishermen.

Rather overwhelmed by all the strangers, Lily was leaning against his leg, nibbling her thumb, and he had a reassuring hand on her head. Every time she saw them close together, a choked feeling clogged Alice's throat and she had to bite her lip.

Roger whistled soundlessly. 'What a change in them both! Is that thanks to you, Alice?'

'They just needed time to get used to each other,' said Alice, but deep down she hoped that she *had* made a difference. At least Will and Lily would have each other from now on.

She would have nobody.

Roger wandered off to have a word with someone he recognized, and Beth turned to Alice with mock reproach. 'We've hardly seen you recently!'

'I know, I'm sorry,' said Alice, guiltily aware that she had been so involved with Will and Lily that she hadn't given her old friends the attention they deserved. 'It's been...busy.'

'Well, as long as you've been having a good time.'

Alice thought about the day out on the reef. About reading with Lily on the verandah. About lying under the ceiling fan with Will breathing quietly beside her, and the thrill of anticipation when he rolled towards her with a smile. To her horror, she felt tears sting her eyes, and she was very glad of her sunglasses.

'Oh, yes,' she said with a careless shrug. 'It's been fun.'

'We wondered if you'd think about staying,' said Beth, ultra-casual. 'You and Will must have got quite close.'

'Yes, it's been nice seeing him again.' Alice was shocked by how unconcerned she could sound when she tried. 'But, you know, when it's time to go…A new nanny is coming out next week, so there's not much point in me staying any longer. Besides, I've still got my ticket home.'

'Oh, you're going?' Beth looked disappointed. 'You will come and see us before you— Oh!' She broke off abruptly and put a hand to her stomach.

'Beth?' said Alice in quick concern. 'Are you all right?'

'Just a bit sick,' muttered Beth, and when Alice looked closely she saw that, beneath her hat, Beth was looking grey and drawn.

'Come inside,' she said, taking Beth's arm. 'It's cooler in there, and you can sit down.'

She made Beth sit in a cool quiet room while she went to find some cold water. 'Shall I get Roger?' she asked worriedly when she came back. It wasn't like Beth to be ill. 'You don't look at all well.'

'I'll be fine in a minute,' said Beth, sipping the water. She smiled at Alice. 'Don't look so worried. It's good news. Oh, Alice, I'm pregnant at last!'

Alice gasped. '*Beth!* That's *fantastic* news!'

'It's early days yet,' Beth warned, 'so we're not telling anyone yet, but I wanted you to know.'

'Oh, Beth …' Tears shone in Alice's eyes as she hugged her friend. 'I won't tell anyone, I promise, but I'm so, so happy for you! And Roger…he must be thrilled!'

'He is. Neither of us can quite believe it yet,' Beth confessed. 'We've wanted this for so long, and we were just beginning to think it wasn't going to happen. Of course, I didn't count on quite how sick I'd feel!'

Alice was so elated by Beth's news that she forgot her own misery about saying goodbye to Will for a while. Leaving Beth to recover in the cool, she sailed out with a wide smile to find Roger.

Roger being Roger, she found him in the middle of a laughing group. Mindful of the need for secrecy, it took all her ingenuity to extricate him but she finally managed to drag him to a quiet place behind the laboratory where she threw her arms around him and promptly burst into tears.

'Hey, what's the matter?' asked Roger in alarm, enveloping her in a comforting hug.

'I'm just so happy for you,' Alice snuffled against his broad chest.

'Ah.' Roger began to smile. 'You've been talking to Beth?'

'Yes, and I'm sworn to secrecy, but it's such fantastic news,' she said, lifting her head to smile at him through her tears. 'I know how much it means to you both.'

'Well, we're expecting you to be godmother, so you'd better come back when the baby is born.'

For a fleeting moment Alice wondered how on earth she would cope with coming back when she would be bound to meet Will again, but she pushed that thought resolutely out of her mind. It was Roger and Beth who mattered now.

'Of course I will,' she told him. 'Try keeping me away from my first godchild!'

She was still smiling when she and Roger rejoined the party. Beth had recovered by then, but Alice was glad to see that Roger took her away soon afterwards. She couldn't help noticing the tender way he put his arm around his wife, and she watched wistfully as he ushered Beth out to the car.

Their devotion to each other brought a lump to Alice's throat. Roger and Beth were lucky. They loved each other completely and they faced everything together. They had had their sadnesses, but their life seemed so much less complicated than her own. Everything was simple for Roger and Beth. Why had she had to fall in love with someone whose life was incompatible with hers?

Sighing, she turned to find Will watching her. His jaw was set and his mouth was pressed together in a decidedly grim line, but Alice's heart still skipped a beat at the sight of him.

'Oh… Hi,' she said.

'You look very sad, Alice,' he said, an edge to his voice that Alice was too full of emotion to analyse.

'I'm not sad,' she said. 'Envious, perhaps.'

'Of Beth?'

'Yes.' She was a little surprised that he had guessed so quickly. 'I think she knows how lucky she is.'

'Does she?'

This time there was no mistaking the hardness in his voice, and Alice looked at him, puzzled. But, before she could ask what he meant, Will's attention was claimed by someone who came up to say goodbye.

The event seemed to be winding down, anyway, and, feeling deflated after the earlier high, she began to help with the clearing up. In spite of her hat, she was beginning to feel the effects of standing in the sun too long, and her head was thumping, so when Will told her that one of the divers had offered her and Lily a lift home she was glad to accept.

'I'll need to wait and lock up when everyone else has gone,' he said brusquely.

Alice had put an exhausted Lily to bed by the time he came back, and she was sitting on the verandah and trying not to think that this time next week she would be home. She tried to imagine herself in her flat. She would pick up the accumulated post from the doormat. She would unpack her case, and put some washing on.

And then what? Desolation washed over her at the realisation that there would be no one to sit down with, no one to have missed her, no one to pour her a drink or put an arm around her and tell her that they were glad she was home. She would be alone again.

'There you are.' Will let the screen door crash behind him. He was carrying a bottle of beer, and although he sat down in his usual chair nothing else was normal. His expression was stony, and he was taut with suppressed feeling, wound up so tight that Alice looked at him in concern. *Something* had obviously happened, but she had the nerve-racking feeling that if she put a foot wrong he would explode.

'Long day,' she ventured cautiously.

'Yes.'

'Still, I think it was a success.'

'Yes.'

There was a pause while Alice eyed him warily. 'Do you want anything to eat?'

'No,' he said, adding grudgingly as Alice raised her brows, 'Thank you.'

'I wasn't hungry either,' she said, and gave up. If Will wanted to tell her what the problem was, he could, but she was in no mood to sit here and coax it out of him if he didn't feel like cooperating. Let him keep it all bottled up inside him, if that was what he wanted.

The silence lengthened uncomfortably. Will drank his beer grimly, until at last he put the bottle down on the table between them with a sharp click.

'I think you should be more careful of Beth's feelings,' he said abruptly.

Alice wasn't sure what she was expecting, but it certainly wasn't that!

'What on earth do you mean?' she asked in astonishment.

'I saw you with Roger this afternoon.'

She stared at him. Surely he wasn't jealous of *Roger*? 'Yes, we're friends. Of course I talked to Roger!'

'What were you talking to him about?'

Opening her mouth to tell him, Alice remembered her promise to Beth just in time and closed it again. 'That's none of your business,' she said after a moment.

'Because *friends* don't usually sneak away behind the lab to have a conversation, or kiss and cuddle each other when they're doing it!'

Will had been gripped by a white-hot fury ever since he had watched Alice drag Roger out of sight. He didn't know what had prompted him to follow them—all right, he did know, he was jealous—but he was completely unprepared for the fist that had closed around his heart as he had seen Alice bury her face in Roger's broad chest and cling to him.

Unable to watch any more, he had turned on his heel and left them to it, and he might have left it at that if he hadn't caught sight of Beth emerging from the office a few minutes later, looking pale and wan. She'd asked him if he had seen Roger, so of course he had said no. He couldn't have her interrupting that scene behind the lab, but, from her drawn look, he couldn't help thinking that she already suspected that something was wrong.

And now Alice wasn't even bothering to deny it.

'Roger and I have always hugged and kissed each other,' she said, her eyes blazing at his tone. 'He's a *friend* and that's what we do. We're not all repressed scientists,' she was unable to resist adding snidely.

'Is Beth a friend too?'

'You know she is.'

'You don't treat her like one,' said Will harshly. 'I saw her today too. She looked wretched, and I'm not surprised, if she has any idea of what you and her husband are up to!'

For a moment, Alice was so outraged that she couldn't speak, could only gulp in disbelief and fury. 'Are you implying that Roger and I are having an affair?' she asked dangerously when she could get the words out.

'I'm saying that you don't behave to him the way you should if you were a good friend to Beth.'

'How dare you!' Alice surged to her feet, shaking with fury. 'I've known Roger for years and there's *never* been anything between us. You should know that better than anyone! I love Roger dearly, but we've never felt like that about each other.'

'Are you sure about that?' Will asked unpleasantly, remembering that disastrous evening when Roger had confessed how he really felt about Alice.

'Yes, I'm sure! And, even if I wasn't, do you really think that I'm the kind of person who would break up a friend's marriage?' She shook her head, unable to believe that Will could be saying such things. 'What do you think I *am*? We've been sleeping together, for God's sake! What did you think, that I was just making do with you because I couldn't have Roger?'

Turning away with an exclamation of disbelief and disgust, she wrapped her arms around her in an attempt to stop herself shaking. 'I suppose you think that after Tony left, I came out here deliberately to ensnare Roger because I didn't have a man of my own!'

'I'm a scientist,' said Will, who didn't believe anything of the kind but who was too angry to think about what he was saying. Seeing Alice with Roger had provided an outlet for all the pent-up anger, confusion and bitterness he had been feeling ever since she had refused to stay, and he wasn't capable of thinking clearly right now. 'I believe the evidence, and I've seen you cuddling up to Roger at every opportunity. You can't tell me that you've never thought what that does to him!'

Alice turned slowly to stare at him. 'I don't believe this,' she said. 'How can you possibly think that about me? You know me!'

'I used to,' he said bleakly. 'I'm not sure I do know you any more.'

There was an appalled silence.

'I think I'd better go,' said Alice in a shaking voice at last, and she turned blindly for the door.

The expression on her face brought Will to his senses too late, and he scrambled to his feet. 'Alice, wait!'

But she only shook her head without looking at him. 'I'll leave tomorrow,' she said, and let the screen door click back into place behind her.

Alice sat carefully down on the back steps next to Lily. She had broken the news at breakfast that she was leaving that day and it had gone even worse than she had feared. Not that Lily had cried or had a tantrum. She had simply stared disbelievingly at Alice out of dark eyes, then had got up without a word and run out into the garden. Heavy hearted, Alice had finished her packing. Now Roger was waiting with a bleak-faced Will by the car, and she had come to try and say goodbye to Lily.

Lily wouldn't acknowledge her presence at first. Her body was rigid, her face averted, and Alice was dismayed to see the closed, blank expression that she remembered from their first meeting.

'Lily,' she began helplessly. 'I'm sorry I have to go like this. I was going anyway in a few days, but I didn't want it to be this way.'

'I don't care,' said Lily, but a spasm crossed her face, and Alice's heart cracked. It wasn't long since this child had lost her mother, and now the next person she had allowed close seemed to be abandoning her too. She tried to put a comforting arm around her, but Lily shook it off.

'Oh, Lily, it's not that I want to leave you,' she sighed.

'Then why are you going? Is it because I've been naughty?'

'Of course not,' said Alice, appalled. 'Of *course* not, Lily. It's nothing to do with you. I wish I could explain but it's…complicated…adult stuff,' she said lamely. She wasn't going to leave Lily thinking that it had anything to do with Will. Her father was the only constant in her life now, and, hurt as Alice was, she wouldn't do anything to jeopardise his relationship with his daughter.

'Helen will be coming soon,' she went on. 'And it'll be difficult for her if I'm still here. I'm going to miss you more than I can say, but you'll like Helen, I promise you.'

'I won't!' Lily jumped furiously to her feet. 'I'll hate her like I hate you!' she shouted, and ran off before Alice could reach out to her.

Unable to keep back the tears any longer, Alice buried her face in her hands and wept.

The screen door creaked, and she could hear steps on the wooden verandah before someone sat down beside her. 'She doesn't hate you,' Will's voice said gently. 'She loves you. She's only angry because you're leaving her, and she doesn't understand why.'

There was a pause, punctuated by Alice's hiccupping sobs.

'I don't have Lily's excuse,' Will went on after a moment. 'I *do* understand why you're going, but I was still angry because I love you, too, and I don't want you to go, even though I know that you must.'

Alice's hands were still covering her face, but her sobs had subsided slightly, and he could tell that she was listening.

'I'm so sorry about last night, Alice,' he said quietly. 'I said some unforgivable things, and I said them because I'm a jealous fool, but really because I was looking for an excuse to hate you, like Lily, because making myself hate you seemed like the only way I could bear the thought of you leaving me.'

Drawing a shuddering breath, Alice lifted her head at last and wiped her eyes with a wobbly thumb. She didn't say anything, but Will was encouraged enough to go on. 'It was a childish reaction, I know, but I haven't been thinking straight recently. I've been flailing round, so wretched and miserable because you were going that I would say anything.

'I lied when I said I didn't know you, Alice,' he said. 'I *do* know you. You're the truest person I know. You would never do anything to hurt Roger or Beth, and I knew it when I was saying it. I just wanted to hurt you so that you felt what I was feeling.'

Alice opened her mouth, but he put a gentle finger on her lips. 'Let me finish. I've made such a bloody mess of everything, Alice. I've hurt you, and because I've hurt you I've hurt Lily, and I don't know how I'm going to forgive myself for either.'

He looked into Alice's golden eyes, puffy now and swimming with tears, but still beautiful. 'I won't ask you again if you'll stay. I know you've got your life to go back to, and goodbyes like these are too hard to go through again. Go with Roger now, and fly home as you planned. I'll look after Lily. She'll be all right.

'I hope you find what you're looking for, Alice,' he went on, although his throat was so tight he had to force the words out. 'I hope you'll be happy, as happy as we were here, and all those years ago. I've always loved you, and I know now that I always will. It's only ever going to be you, Alice,' he said with an unsteady smile. 'I want you to know that if you ever change your mind, and think you can take a chance on being loved utterly and completely, Lily and I will be here for you, and we'll take as much or as little as you can give.'

'Will...I...I don't know what to say,' said Alice hopelessly.

'You don't need to say anything.' Will put a hand under her

elbow and helped her to her feet. 'You need to go home and decide for yourself what you really want, without me shouting at you and Lily piling on the emotional blackmail!'

'Tell Lily …' Alice's voice cracked and she couldn't go on, but Will seemed to understand what she needed to say.

'I'll explain why you're going,' he said. 'I'll tell her that you know that she doesn't really hate you, and that you love her too.'

'Thank you,' she whispered. She didn't seem to be able to stop crying as she walked through the screen door for the last time and out to the front where Roger was waiting by the car.

'Come on then, waterworks,' he said gruffly. 'I've got your cases.'

'Alice,' said Will as she was about to get into the passenger seat, and she paused, a hand on the door and one foot in the well. 'Thank you,' he said simply. 'Thank you for everything you've done for Lily, and for me.'

Unable to speak, she nodded.

'And remember what I said about being here if you ever change your mind,' he added, his voice strained, and Alice bit her lip to stop the tears spilling over once more.

'I will,' she said. Then she ducked her head as she got into the car and closed the door, and Will could only watch in desolation as Roger drove her away.

CHAPTER TEN

THERE was so much post piled up behind the front door that Alice had to push her way into her cramped hallway. The flat smelt musty and unused, and even when she had switched on the lights the rooms seemed cheerless. Perhaps it was something to do with the dreary drizzle and the muted grey light of a wet Spring afternoon, she thought, and tried not to think of the aching blue ocean, the mint-green lagoon and the vivid colours of hibiscus and bougainvillaea.

Her feet had swollen on the long flight, and she kicked off her shoes with a weary sigh as she sat down on the cream sofa. This was the home she had worked hard for, the home she had been insistent she wanted to come back to. It represented everything she had ever wanted: security, stability, being settled at last. She had decorated it with care in the cool, minimalist style that appealed to her, and it had been her refuge whenever things had gone wrong.

Until now, she had always thought of her home as calm and restful. There was no reason suddenly to find the ivory walls cold, or to notice the roar of the traffic along the busy road outside, the dismaying wail of a siren in the distance, and the intrusive blare of a television next door.

No reason to find herself overwhelmed with homesickness

for a verandah thousands of miles away, where the insects whirred and rasped and shrilled, and the scent of frangipani drifted on the hot air. Alice looked at her watch and calculated the time in St Bonaventure. Will would be sitting there now, still and self-contained, listening to the sound of the sea he loved so much.

The memory of him was so sharp that Alice closed her eyes as if at a pain. Was he thinking of her? Was he missing her?

She had thought about him constantly since Roger had driven her away. The worst thing was realising that she hadn't said goodbye, to him or to Lily.

His words went round and round in her head. It's only ever going to be you, Alice. Lily and I will be here for you if you ever change your mind and think you can take a chance on being loved…

'I don't understand what the problem is,' Beth had said. 'Why are you putting yourself through all this misery? Will loves you, Lily loves you, and you wouldn't be this upset about leaving if you didn't love them back.'

'Love's not the problem,' Alice had tried to explain.

'Then what is?'

'It's everything else. It's not being sure if love would be enough.' She'd twisted her fingers in an agony of indecision. 'Yes, I could go back to Will now, but it would mean giving up my whole life for something that might not work out. It didn't work out last time, so why should it now?'

'You know yourselves better now,' Beth had pointed out, but Alice hadn't been convinced.

'I'm not sure that I do. I feel differently here,' she'd said, waving her arms at the tropical garden. 'But who's to say that what I feel is real? It might just be about being on holiday in a beautiful place. Maybe I'm just getting carried away by the romance of it all.'

Beth had looked thoughtful. 'Then perhaps Will is right. You need to go home and see how you feel when you're there. He's told you that he loves you, and he's not going anywhere, so it's up to you to decide what you want.'

It was deciding that was the problem, Alice thought in despair. She who had always been so clear about what she wanted before was now being tossed about in a maelstrom of indecision that was making her feel quite sick. One minute the thought of never seeing or touching Will again seemed so awful that she was ready to jump into a taxi and rush back to the house by the lagoon, the next she would think about selling her flat and committing herself to an expatriate life where they would move from house to house and none of them would be a home. And she would be swamped by memories of her childhood and all the times she had sworn that as soon as she was old enough she would settle down and make a home for herself.

She wasn't ready to give that up, Alice told herself. At least, she didn't think she was …

She was having to readjust so many of her ideas at the moment, that it was difficult to know *what* she thought. She had been astounded when Beth had told her just why Will had been so convinced that her relationship with Roger was inappropriate.

'It's not so far-fetched an idea,' Beth had said. 'Roger was in love with you for years.'

'What?' Alice had goggled at her, and Beth had nodded calmly.

'He confessed to Will once when he'd had too much to drink, and he was always grateful that Will never told you. He thought it would have embarrassed you if you'd known.'

'But I… But I …' Alice had floundered in disbelief. 'I had no *idea*!'

'Roger knew that. He'd probably have been better to have

told you and got you out of his system, but you know what fools men can be about these things,' said Roger's fond wife.

Alice regarded her curiously. 'Didn't you mind when he told you?' she asked a little awkwardly, not at all sure it wasn't a bit tacky to ask a man's wife how she felt when she'd found out he was in love with you.

'No,' said Beth, smiling. 'He told me that when he met me he realised that what he'd felt for you wasn't the real thing, and I believe him. I know Roger loves me, Alice. He loves you too, but in a very different way. I've always been sure of that.'

'It must be nice to be so sure,' said Alice wistfully, and then her face darkened as she remembered Will's bitter accusations. 'I can see why Will might be suspicious, I suppose, but it doesn't change the fact that he actually thought me capable of coming out here and making a play for Roger.'

Beth sighed. 'He apologised for that, didn't he? The man's desperate, Alice! If you won't go and see him, will you at least ring him?'

But Alice shook her head. 'It wouldn't be fair to do that until I was sure, the way you're sure about Roger, and I'm not. Helen's arriving today. It would just upset everyone if I went back now. My flight's tomorrow, and we'd just end up having to say goodbye all over again. No, I'm going to go home, and when I can think clearly again maybe I'll know how I feel.'

It was all very well deciding to think about her situation clearly, but it wasn't that easy in practice. Alice was convinced that all she needed was a good night's sleep and to wake up in her flat and suddenly she would know what to do, but it didn't work like that.

She did her best to get back into a routine as quickly as possible. She unpacked, shook the sand out of her shoes, washed and put away her holiday clothes and set about finding a new job. She filled in application forms, bought herself a smart new suit for interviews, and contacted friends she hadn't seen before the break-up with Tony.

Grimly determined to enjoy herself if it killed her, she went out as much as she could. Once she bumped into Tony and Sandi, and was appalled to discover how indifferent she felt as the three of them made polite chit-chat. She had been sure that Tony was the man she wanted to spend the rest of her life with, but how could she have wanted him when he didn't have Will's mouth or Will's smile or Will's ironic grey eyes? But, if her feelings towards him could change so completely in a matter of months, who was to say that her feelings for Will wouldn't change too?

So Alice continued, miserably unsure, torn between her determination to get back into her old life and her inability to put her time in St Bonaventure out of her mind. She would be sitting having coffee with a friend, and her eyes would slip out of focus momentarily at the memory of Will's hands around a mug. She let herself into the flat, and found herself listening for the click of the screen door, and if she caught a glimpse of a dark-haired little girl her heart would lurch with the bizarre hope that it was Lily.

She ached for Will, for his cool, quiet presence, his wry smile and his hard body. She missed the constant sigh of the sea and the soughing of the warm wind in the palm trees. She missed the hot nights. She missed Lily desperately, but most of all she missed Will.

Alice longed to hear from him. Every time she went home, she would check for an email, a message on the answering machine, a postcard, anything to show that he was still thinking about her. There was never anything. *You need to go home and decide for yourself.* She could still hear Will saying it, and she wanted to shout at him that she *couldn't* decide.

If only he would make some move, it would take nothing to convince her. Why didn't he just contact her?

She began to set herself little tests. If she could get through the morning without thinking about him, that must mean that she was getting over him, and then she'd know she'd made the right decision. If she hadn't heard from him by next week, she'd know he didn't really care and that it wasn't meant to be. If she could walk to the end of the street without stepping on the cracks in the pavement, she'd be able to make up her mind.

None of them worked.

When her dream job was advertised in the trade journal, Alice could hardly believe it. This, surely, was the sign that she had been waiting for. The job was everything she'd ever wanted. A prestigious company, a promotion, a challenging position that would launch her into a new stage of her career. If she got this job, she was meant to stay in London and get on with her life. What could be clearer?

Carefully, Alice filled in the application form, and when she passed the first hurdle and was asked for interview she had her suit cleaned, and bought a spectacular pair of new shoes to go with it. She prepared for the interview as thoroughly as she could, but she was very nervous as she waited to go in. It felt as if her whole future would be decided by that hour's interview.

Her shoes pinched horribly, but otherwise it seemed to go quite well, and then all Alice had to do was wait.

When her phone rang a few hours later, she practically jumped out of her skin. She had spent the afternoon prowling restlessly about the flat, unable to settle to anything. Too jittery to take off her suit, she was barefoot on the carpet, her poor toes enjoying a respite from being pushed into the shoes that might look fabulous but were in fact extremely uncomfortable.

This was it. Alice stared at the ringing phone for a moment and then picked it up. 'Hello?'

'Ms Gunning?' said a voice she recognized from the interview that morning. 'Thank you so much for coming to see us this morning. We're absolutely delighted to offer you the post.'

The rest of the conversation was a blur of congratulations, but it finished with a suggestion that she go in and see them the next day to sort out the practicalities of salary and starting date. In the meantime, they would courier over her contract so that she could read it at her leisure.

'Thank you so much.' Alice put the phone down slowly.

So the job was hers. Finally her decision had been made for her. She was to stay here, with a great job, a nice flat, and friends. She had a good life, and she was safe and settled again, just as she had always wanted.

She was ecstatically happy and relieved, naturally.

She burst into tears.

Aghast at herself, Alice sank on to the sofa, brushing the tears angrily from her face. What on earth was the matter with her? She had wanted a sign, and this was it. She should be delighted, not sick to her stomach with disappointment.

But, the more she tried to convince herself that she had got what she wanted, the more she cried, until her face was blotched and piggy, and her throat was clogged with sobs.

As if that wasn't enough, the doorbell pealed imperatively. 'Oh, God, now what?' mumbled Alice. She didn't want to explain her wretched state to a neighbour, and she was in no mood for a survey, but it might be the contract. She would have to check.

Cautiously, she put her eye to the peephole and peered through the door. If it was a courier, she would open the door, take the contract and close it again. If it was a friend or a neighbour, she would just have to pretend that she wasn't there.

But it wasn't a friend or a neighbour, or a market researcher, or even a courier. Standing on the other side of the door were the very last people she had expected to see.

Her parents.

Alice was humming as she jumped off the bus and walked back to the flat past the little parade of shops. She waved at the owner of the Turkish greengrocer, and the young boy who helped at the Indian corner shop that sold everything she could ever want in the middle of the night. Stopping at the street market, she bought a bunch of hyacinths, and sniffed appreciatively as she passed an Italian restaurant where something very garlicky was cooking. Two elderly ladies swathed in black were coming towards her, deep in conversation, and Alice smiled as she stood aside for them.

She loved this multi-cultural side to London. The city was looking at its best in the spring sunshine. In the centre of town, the great parks were green and bright with flowers nodding gaily in the breeze, and the very air seemed sharper and clearer, as if the world was conspiring to reassure her that she had made the right decision. Even the bus had come just when she wanted it, and she had enjoyed the ride on the top deck back to her suburb. It might not be as attractive as the centre of town, but it had its own vibrancy and charm. Yes, this was a great city to live in.

Alice couldn't believe how much better she felt for making up her mind. Filled with a sense of well-being, she was smiling as she turned into her street, and it wasn't until she was halfway along that she saw that someone was standing on her doorstep. Someone whose shape and stance was achingly familiar.

Her steps slowed in disbelief, until she stopped altogether with her hand on the gate, her smile fading. He turned at her approach, and as they looked at each other the beat of the great metropolis, the jabber of languages, the constant throb of traffic, the rattle of trains, the blare of music, and the car alarm that everyone was ignoring, faded into a blur. And then silence, until there was just the two of them, looking at each other.

Will.

Alice drank in the sight of him. He looked tired, she thought, but it was unmistakably him. It was as if a high-definition lens had been slotted over her eyes so that she could see him in extraordinary detail: every line around his eyes, every crease in his cheek, the way his hair grew, the set of his mouth…

Oh, that mouth… Her knees went suddenly weak, and she had to hang on to the gate.

'Hello,' she said.

'Hello, Alice.'

He didn't smile, he didn't rush to sweep her into his arms, he just stood there and looked directly back at her. But that was the moment nonetheless when the last piece clicked into place for Alice, and she realised that she wasn't even surprised to see him. All that misery, all that indecision, all that dithering…all had led inevitably to this time and this place, to this certainty that everything would be all right.

Discovering that she was able to move after all, Alice pushed open the gate and pulled out her keys as she walked towards him.

'Have you been waiting long?'

'About forty minutes.'

About ten years, Will amended to himself.

Alice looked wonderful. The mere sight of her was enough to lift his heart, but he was conscious of a sinking sense of consternation too. Part of him, *admit it,* had hoped that she would have been wretched and miserable without him, and that it would have showed, but there was no evidence of that. Instead, she looked glowing and confident in a short jacket with a long flowing skirt and boots, and flowers in her arms. Her hair fell to her shoulders, and when she stood at the gate it shone gold and copper and bronze in the spring light, and her eyes were full of sunshine.

She looked happy, Will realised dully, and he was terribly afraid that he had left it too late.

Alice went into the kitchen and put the hyacinths into some water, bending to breathe in their heady perfume. 'Coffee?' she asked.

'Thanks.' Will wasn't sure how to begin. He stood to one side and watched her moving around the kitchen. She hadn't asked what he was doing there, but presumably she could guess, and surely they had known each other long enough for him not to need to dance around with polite conversation before coming to the point?

'I've been wondering if you'd thought at all about what I said before you left,' he said abruptly. 'Have you decided what you want yet?'

Alice had sat on a chair and was pulling off her boots, but she stopped in the middle of unzipping the second one and smiled at him. 'Yes,' she said. 'Yes, I have.'

'I see,' said Will bleakly. She had decided to stay in London, that was obvious. You didn't buy flowers for a home you were about to leave.

'Shall we go into the sitting room?' Alice suggested before he could say any more, and she carried the tray into a bright room. It was cool and uncluttered, and Will sat gingerly on the edge of a cream sofa. She looked perfectly at home here. If this was her life, he wasn't surprised that she hadn't wanted to give it up for a rickety verandah and creaking ceiling fans.

Alice pushed the plunger into the cafetière and poured out the coffee, wriggling her toes on the carpet. Will was so used to seeing her in shoes that the sight of her bare feet was strangely arousing, and he looked away.

'What are you doing here, Will?' she asked as she handed him a mug of coffee. 'I thought you were going to wait for me to decide what I wanted to do?'

'I was going to—I *meant* to wait—but there came a point when I couldn't wait any longer.' Will put down his coffee without drinking it. 'It's terrible since you left, Alice,' he told her honestly. 'Lily has closed in on herself again.'

Alice bit her lip. 'Doesn't she get on with Helen?'

'Helen's all right. She's done her best. It's not her fault that she's not you,' said Will. 'The truth is that Lily and I are in a bad way. I can't sleep, I can't eat, I can't work properly… We don't seem to be able to do anything but miss you.'

A wry smile touched his mouth. 'I know this sounds like emotional blackmail, Alice, but it's not meant to be that. It's just that it suddenly seemed stupid to just sit out there and hope for the best. I couldn't just watch my daughter getting quieter and quieter. I realised that if we wanted you back in our lives—and we do—I would have to do something to make it happen.

'So I've applied for a job here in the UK,' he told Alice. 'It's as a consultant with an engineering company, doing environmental impact assessments for their marine projects. I'd be based in the North, not London, but it's a permanent job, and a good one. I'd still have to do research overseas, but it would be in short stints, so we could buy a house and settle down somewhere. Lily could go to school, and you could carry on with your career …'

Will stopped, realising that he was in danger of babbling. He looked at Alice, who was clasping her mug with a very strange expression on her face, as if she couldn't quite believe what she was hearing.

'I suppose what I really came to ask you, Alice, was

whether it would make any difference to your decision if I did get that job.'

Very slowly, Alice shook her head. 'No,' she said. 'No, it wouldn't make any difference.'

'I see.' The belief that deep down Alice still loved him had been keeping Will going through the last ghastly weeks. He knew that she was scarred by her restless childhood and he knew how important the idea of home was to her. Once he had made the decision to change his own career, he had thought that would solve the problem, but he could see now that it had been arrogant of him. Alice had never promised anything beyond the short term.

Somehow he managed a smile. 'I understand,' he said. 'Now that I've seen you here, I can appreciate what this place means to you.' He looked around the room, approving its simple, tasteful décor. 'It's nice here. You've obviously got a good life, and I know how important your career is to you. I hope you'll find just the job you want,' he added heroically.

'It's funny you should say that,' said Alice, a smile hovering around her mouth. 'I was offered the job of my dreams just a couple of days ago.'

'Well...great,' said Will heartily. Abandoning his coffee, he got to his feet. He wasn't sure how he was going to tell Lily, but he would have to find a way. She had been happy to see her grandparents again. Perhaps he should think about moving to the UK anyway, just as Alice had once suggested. 'Good luck then, Alice.'

'Where are you going?'

'I should go and pick Lily up. It was good to see you again,' he said, looking into Alice's golden eyes for the last time. 'And... Well, there doesn't seem much more to say.'

He was turning for the door when her soft voice stopped him in his tracks. 'Even if I tell you that I didn't take the job?'

Very, very slowly, Will turned back. 'You didn't take it?'

Alice shook her head, her smile a little wavery. 'You haven't asked me what decision I made yet,' she reminded him.

'I thought...I assumed ...' he stammered as a tiny spark of hope lit in his heart. 'You look so happy, so at home here.'

She tutted. 'That's not very scientific of you, Will. I'd have expected you to look at the evidence, not make assumptions on how you think I look.'

'Evidence?'

Getting to her feet, Alice went over to the table and rummaged among some papers, pulling out a rectangular card. 'Evidence like this,' she said, putting it into a flabbergasted Will's hand. 'It's a plane ticket,' she told him unnecessarily. 'Open it.'

'It's to St Bonaventure.' Will lifted his head from the ticket to stare at her, a smile starting at the back of his eyes.

'And it's in my name.' She took the ticket from him and tossed it back onto the table before turning back to him and taking his hand, smiling as his fingers closed convulsively around hers. 'What does that evidence tell you, Will?'

'Alice ...' Unable to find the words for how he felt, Will pulled her into his arms. He didn't kiss her, he just held her very tightly, his eyes squeezed shut, his face pressed into her hair as he breathed in the scent of her, and felt the iron bands that had been gripped around his heart ever since she had driven off with Roger start to loosen.

'I made my decision, Will.' Alice turned her face into his throat and clung to him. 'I chose happiness. I chose you.'

Will's arms tightened around her even further, but she didn't mind. 'You were right about me looking happy,' she went on, rather muffled. 'I was happy because I'd just finished making all the arrangements to let this flat and could go back to you and Lily.'

'But Alice, this is your home,' Will protested.

'It was, but when I came back from St Bonaventure it wasn't home any more,' she said. 'It was just a flat. For a while it seemed as if I didn't have a home at all, and then I realised that I do. It's just not bricks and mortar. Home is wherever you are.'

'Alice... Oh, Alice ...' Will pulled back slightly so that she could turn her face up to his, and their lips met at last in a long, sweet kiss. He felt almost drunk with relief and happiness. He wasn't sure quite how it happened, but his dream had just come true, and the proof of it was Alice's lips beneath his, her arms around him, the softness and scent of her hair. 'Tell me that again,' he said raggedly when they broke for air.

'I love you, Will. I think I've always loved you, but I was too stupid and afraid to realise how lucky I was to have found you.' Lovingly, she traced the line of his cheek with her fingers. 'I've walked away from your love three times now, and I don't deserve to be given another chance, but, if you will, I promise I'll never walk away again. I just want to be with you, and I don't care where we are, or what we do, as long as we're together.'

'And you're sure?' asked Will as he bent to kiss her again, and she smiled against his lips.

'Yes, this time I'm sure.'

'What made you change your mind?' Will asked much later when they were lying, lazily entangled, in Alice's bed. He smoothed the hair tenderly from her face. 'You were so insistent that you had everything you needed here.'

'Everything except you and Lily,' said Alice, rolling onto her side to face him. 'It didn't take me long to realise that I might have the security of material things, but none of them were worth anything without you. I knew I loved you, and that you loved me, but I still couldn't bring myself to trust that feeling.

'I was afraid to let go of what I had,' she confessed. 'It was just what you said. I was afraid to give it all up for the chance of happiness.' She linked her fingers with his. 'Once you know what you want, it all seems obvious, and I can't believe now that I hesitated for so long. But then I was going round and round in circles, not knowing what I wanted or what I really thought.

'Strangely, it was being offered that job that convinced me,' she remembered. 'I'd told myself that I would take it as a sign that I should stay here if I got it, but of course, when it happened, I realised it wasn't the sign I wanted. I felt a fool,' she told him with a twisted smile. 'I'd just been offered the job of my dreams, and all I could think was that I didn't want it if it meant I couldn't be with you and Lily. Then my parents turned up.'

'Your parents?' Will sat up in surprise. 'I thought they were in India?'

'They were. Now they're on their way to keep bees in Normandy.' Out of habit, Alice rolled her eyes, but her smile held a kind of wry affection as well. 'They thought they would call in and see me on their way through London, and, being them, they didn't think to give me any warning. They simply turned up on my doorstep, at the very moment I'd just realised that I wanted to be with you, and I was in a terrible muddle about everything.'

Will twisted a strand of her hair around his finger. 'Did they help?'

'Well, that's the funny thing. They did.' Alice pulled herself up to sit next to him, and adjusted a pillow behind her back. 'They've never been what you'd call conventional parents. They're two old hippies,' she said with an affectionate smile, thinking of her mother with her anklets and long braid, her father with his tie-dyed T-shirt and his grey hair pulled back into a pony-tail. 'But when they saw what a state I was in, they swung into their traditional roles straight away! They sat me down and made me tea, and got the whole story out of me.'

She ran her hand over Will's shoulder, loving the sleekness of his skin. 'I told them about you and Lily, and how much I loved you, and that I'd let you down three times now. I told them I was afraid of doing it again, that I was scared that it wouldn't work unless I was sure that I could get it right this time and that it would be perfect.'

Her mother had simply shaken her head. 'Alice, you can never be sure,' she had said. 'All you can do is trust each other and be true to each other and believe in each other. Love isn't something that comes and goes. It's something you have to make together, and if you both work at it, if you're kind and patient and prepared to compromise, if you can stay friends through thick and thin, then you can make it last, but you can't *ever* be sure of it.'

Alice would never forget the way her mother had smiled at her father then, and suddenly they hadn't seemed like faintly ridiculous hangovers from another era, but two people who had found their own way and loved each other a long time.

'Loving someone completely isn't easy,' her father had added. 'It's hard work, and you can decide it's easier never to try, but, if you never do, you'll never be completely happy either.' He'd reached out and took her mother's hand. 'Yes, it's a risk committing yourself to loving someone for the rest of your life. It's a leap in the dark, but it's a leap out of the dark too, and if you don't take it you'll never know the joy and the wonder and the real security which is loving and being loved.'

Alice felt quite teary with emotion as she told Will what her parents had said. 'As I listened to them talk, I realised that I'd spent my whole life running away from the unsettling effects of my childhood—the moving from place to place, never having any real friends, never feeling at home—when I could have been thinking about all the wonderful things my parents did for me.'

She shook her head at herself. 'They gave me the best example I could have of a loving relationship. My father didn't wear a suit, and my mother didn't put on an apron and stay in the kitchen, but they were always friends and always lovers. They laughed and they talked and were true to each other. They took me to places most children never get to see, and showed me how wonderful the world is.

'I had the most incredible experiences growing up,' Alice remembered. 'But, instead of realising how lucky I was, I turned it all into something negative. I became afraid of change, and I confused the security of place with the security of love.' She curved her hand around his cheek and leaned over to kiss Will's mouth softly. 'I won't do that again.'

'Your parents sound like great people,' said Will when he had kissed her back. Alice had never talked much about her parents when they'd been students. He had the feeling they had been in South America then, so he had never been introduced. 'I'd like to meet them.'

'That's good, because they're coming out to St Bonaventure.'

'They are? When?'

'For our wedding,' said Alice calmly, and a smile twitched the corner of Will's mouth.

'Oh, we're getting married, are we?'

'Yes, we are.' She leant over to Will until he slid beneath her, and her face was suddenly serious. 'You've asked me to marry you four times now, and each time I've been the fool that said no, so this time it's up to me. Will you marry me, Will?'

'Alice.' He cupped her face with infinite tenderness. 'My heart, I've wanted to marry you since I first laid eyes on you fourteen years ago, but we don't have to get married if you don't want to.'

'I do want to,' she said, dropping soft kisses over his face. 'You know what a thing I've got about security, and, now I've decided that you're my security, I want to tie you up as close as I can!'

'The tying up bit sounds fun,' mumbled Will between kisses. 'You can tie me up as tight as you like!'

'Good, I hoped you'd agree,' said Alice with satisfaction, and then her blizzard of kisses had reached his mouth and neither of them said anything more for a long time.

'We don't have to get married in St Bonaventure,' Will pointed out some time later, when they had both discovered that they were starving and were in the kitchen making cheese on toast, which was the best Alice could do. 'If I get this job, we'll be moving back to the UK and we could have the wedding here if you like.'

Alice picked a piece of cheese from the grater and studied him. 'When's the interview?'

'The day after tomorrow.'

'I think you should ring up and cancel,' she said. 'Let's go back to St Bonaventure and finish the project. If I'm married to you, I'll be able to find a job doing something, and as long as I've got something to do I'll be fine. I could sort out your fund-raising for a start! Then, when the project's finished, we can think again. Maybe that'll be the time to come back to the UK, and Lily can settle in a school here.'

Will slid his arms about her from behind and kissed the side of her neck, making her arch with pleasure. 'You're a dream come true,' he said, and she smiled.

'That's the plan.'

The sun was just starting to sink towards the horizon as Alice took Lily's hand and walked down the garden and across the track. Ducking under the trunk of a coconut palm that leant down at an extraordinary angle, they kicked off their shoes and walked barefoot across the beach to where Will was waiting for them.

Lily was in a pale pink dress, which she had been allowed to choose herself, and her dark curls were held in place by a satin headband decorated with rosebuds. Her tongue was sticking out slightly as she concentrated on remembering her bridesmaid's duties. Next to her, Alice was wearing a very simple cream-coloured dress with fine straps that left her arms and shoulders bare, and the chiffon stirred against her legs as cat's paw of wind ruffled across the lagoon. There were frangipani flowers in her hair, and she carried a spray of vivid bougainvillaea.

The sky was flushed with a pink that was deepening rapidly to a brief blaze of red and orange as Will turned to watch them walk across the sand towards him, and he smiled. Their plans for a small ceremony had been overtaken by the insistence of the entire project staff on being invited, together with Roger and Beth, Alice's parents, his mother, Sara and a whole lot of other people who'd seemed so genuinely happy for them that it had seemed churlish not to include them in the wedding party too. They all gathered round as Will stood with Alice and Lily before the celebrant.

Alice bent and handed her flowers to Lily, who took them as if they were made of glass and stepped carefully back to join her grandmother. Will took Alice's hand and, as they turned to face each other, his grey gaze travelled lovingly over her, from the tawny hair to those golden eyes and the warm, generous mouth, and then down over the enticing curves of her body to stop at her bare feet.

'What, no shoes?' he murmured as the celebrant cleared his throat. 'How are you going to run away?'

She smiled back at him. 'I'm not running anywhere,' she said. 'From now on I'm staying right by your side.'

* * * * *

Turn the page for a sneak preview of
IF I'D NEVER KNOWN YOUR LOVE
by
Georgia Bockoven

From the brand-new series
Harlequin Everlasting Love
Every great love has a story to tell.™

One year, five months and four days missing

There's no way for you to know this, Evan, but I haven't written to you for a few months. Actually, it's been almost a year. I had a hard time picking up a pen once more after we paid the second ransom and then received a letter saying it wasn't enough. I was so sure you were coming home that I took the kids along to Bogotá so they could fly home with you and me, something I swore I'd never do. I've fallen in love with Colombia and the people who've opened their hearts to me. But fear is a constant companion when I'm there. I won't ever expose our children to that kind of danger again.

I'm at a loss over what to do anymore, Evan. I've begged and pleaded and thrown temper tantrums with every official I can corner both here and at home.

They've been incredibly tolerant and understanding, but in the end as ineffectual as the rest of us.

I try to imagine what your life is like now, what you do every day, what you're wearing, what you eat. I want to believe that the people who have you are misguided yet kind, that they treat you well. It's how I survive day to day. To think of you being mistreated hurts too much. If I picture you locked away somewhere and suffering, a weight descends on me that makes it almost impossible to get out of bed in the morning.

Your captors surely know you by now. They have to recognize what a good man you are. I imagine you working with their children, telling them that you have children, too, showing them the pictures you carry in your wallet. Can't the men who have you understand how much your children miss you? How can it not matter to them?

How can they keep you away from us all this time? Over and over, we've done what they asked. Are they oblivious to the depth of their cruelty? What kind of people are they that they don't care?

I used to keep a calendar beside our bed next to the peach rose you picked for me before you left. Every night I marked another day, counting how many you'd been gone. I don't do that any longer. I don't want to be reminded of all the days we'll never get back.

When I can't sleep at night, I tell you about my day. I imagine you hearing me and smiling over the details that make up my life now. I never tell you how defeated I feel at moments or how hard I work to hide it from everyone for fear they will see it as a reason to stop believing you are coming home to us.

And I couldn't tell you about the lump I found in my

breast and how difficult it was going through all the tests without you here to lean on. The lump was benign—the process reaching that diagnosis utterly terrifying. I couldn't stop thinking about what would happen to Shelly and Jason if something happened to me.

We need you to come home.

I'm worn down with missing you.

I'm going to read this tomorrow and will probably tear it up or burn it in the fireplace. I don't want you to get the idea I ever doubted what I was doing to free you or thought the work a burden. I would gladly spend the rest of my life at it, even if, in the end, we only had one day together.

You are my life, Evan.

I will love you forever.

* * * * *

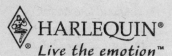

Coming Next Month

#3943 RAISING THE RANCHER'S FAMILY Patricia Thayer
Rocky Mountain Brides
New York tycoon Holt Rawlins is back home in Destiny to find the truth, not to make friends. But when beautiful Leah Keenan bursts into his life, Holt finds he cannot let her go. Leah knows that soon she will have to return to her old life, but to leave Holt will break her heart. Will the rugged rancher persuade her to stay?

#3944 MATRIMONY WITH HIS MAJESTY Rebecca Winters
By Royal Appointment
Darrell Collier is an ordinary single mom. Alexander Valleder is a good, responsible king. But one night, years ago, he rebelled a little. The result, as he's just discovered, was a child. Now Alex has to sweep Darrell off her feet and persuade her that she has the makings of a queen.

#3945 THE SHEIKH'S RELUCTANT BRIDE Teresa Southwick
Desert Brides
Jessica Sterling has just discovered that in the desert kingdom of Bha'Khar is the man that she has been betrothed to since birth! Sheikh Kardhal Hourani is rich, gorgeous and arrogant. Can Jessica see the man behind the playboy persona and find her way into his guarded heart?

#3946 IN THE HEART OF THE OUTBACK... Barbara Hannay
Byrne Drummond has every reason to hate Fiona McLaren—her reckless brother destroyed his family. But the image of Byrne has been etched in Fiona's mind ever since she first saw the stoic, broad-shouldered cattleman. And Fiona's touch is the first to draw him in years.

#3947 MARRIAGE FOR BABY Melissa McClone
Career-driven couple Jared and Katie have separated. But when they find themselves guardians of an orphaned baby they agree to give their marriage another go for the sake of the child. Little do they know how much this tiny baby will turn their lives—and marriage—upside down.

#3948 RESCUED: MOTHER-TO-BE Trish Wylie
Baby on Board
Colleen McKenna knew that she would have to be strong to cope with her pregnancy alone. But now gorgeous millionaire Eamonn Murphy's kindness is testing her fierce independence. And having Eamonn share each tiny kick with her makes each moment more special than the last.

HRCNM0307